HELLFIRE CLUB - DARLINGTON
AN IMMORTAL WARRIORS NOVEL
Copyright © 2019 by Sara MacKenzie
9780648591177

This is a work of fiction. Names, characters, places and inci-
dents are either the product of the author's imagination or
are used fictitiously, and any resemblance to actual persons,
living or dead, business establishments, events or locales is
entirely coincidental.

Printed in the USA.

Cover Design and Interior Format

© KILLION
THE GROUP INC.

HELLFIRE CLUB: DARLINGTON

AN IMMORTAL WARRIORS NOVEL

SARA MACKENZIE

My dedicated Sara Mackenzie fans,
this one is for you!!

Prologue

1808, Hellfire Club,
Blackfriars Abbey,
Lincolnshire, England

NICHOLAS DARLINGTON WATCHED AS HIS friend Lorne was laid in the ground beside the Destroyer, the demon they had set loose upon an unsuspecting world. It happened so swiftly—one moment Lorne was alive and speaking, and the next he was asleep in the earth, the green grass undisturbed above him.

"We were all in it together!" The words were forced out of him, his hand pressed to the ache in his ribs.

Sutcliffe muttered a curse. "He's right. We called up the demon together. Lorne shouldn't suffer the blame alone."

The Sorceress turned her azure eyes to Darlington and his head swam. He wanted to drop to his knees and beg for mercy, but pride kept him upright.

"Nicholas," she sighed with infinite disappointment.

His injured leg trembled so badly he thought he was going to fall. Sutcliffe's large hand closed on his arm and held him up, although he was shaking too.

"Why did you let the Marquis of Lorne lead you into this terrible mess? You are an intelligent man with a mind of your own. Instead you chose to blunt your senses with wine and willing flesh, and allow yourself to be taken down paths you now regret. Oh, you do regret them, I can see that you do, though your loyalty to your friend keeps you from saying the words."

She leaned in close. He didn't see her move, only felt the immense power radiating from her. Like iron spikes it tore at his flesh and bones, spilling blood he could not see. "You might be a leader of men, Nicholas."

"No," he said, his voice hoarse.

She stared at him a moment longer. "I wonder if you're even able to be saved. Lorne, selfish as he is, has always shown glimpses of the sort of man he could be. Sutcliffe here … well, we shall see. But you, Nicholas? Your crime was dreadful indeed, and instead of attempting to make reparations, you have instead sought to sink further into the mire, and hide your memories in drunken revelry."

His crime *was* dreadful. The scar on his face and his twisted leg were well deserved, but as penance they weren't enough. Not nearly enough. He could never forgive himself, and the only way he could forget was to drink and carouse with his friends. The Hellfire Club served that purpose.

"You're right," he said. "I cannot be saved. Kill me now and set my friends free. I will take their punishment as well as my own."

The Sorceress smiled. "Ah, *now* you give me hope. I don't think I will give up on you just yet, Nicholas."

He wanted to protest but he was already close to fainting. Nicholas Darlington closed his eyes. The world was spinning, and his leg finally gave way. Strangely he didn't fall. He floated down, down into darkness.

Into blessed oblivion.

Chapter One

Present day
Glasgow, Scotland

LINNY MCNAB SMILED ABOUT HER at the circle of expectant faces. Her group was assembled and she was preparing to lead them into the night, and hopefully scare them witless. Well, she had some experience of that, at least.

"Everyone ready?"

Heads nodded and a youngish girl in a long, knitted coat gave an elaborate shiver. "Do you think we'll see any ghosts tonight?" she asked, her American accent making her stand out from the others.

Linny shrugged but raised her eyebrows at the same time, as if to say 'we're about to find out'. They would be walking down some of Glasgow's oldest streets, the ones spared from the bombings of the Second World War and the bulldozers of the nineteen seventies. Who knew what they might find? Though in her experience, anything ghostly had more to do with the over active imaginations of her tour groups than it had a basis in reality.

But who could blame them? It was dark and chilly, and the stories she told were designed to frighten people. She wouldn't be complaining if someone *did* claim to see a ghost. At least then the others would feel like they got their money's worth.

"This way then!" she called, and set out, digging her gloved hands into the pockets of her jacket.

A middle aged man, who had been giving her the eye ever since he arrived, was soon at her side. "Do you believe in ghosts?" he asked. He was probably lonely. A stranger in a strange city looking to hook up. Shame he'd chosen her—a shame for him, that was.

She gave him the standard reply. "Of course I believe in ghosts!" The company she worked for insisted they all be believers. What they didn't know was that Linny believed in far worse things than just ghosts. She'd seen such horrors first hand when a demon called the Destroyer took over her body. She'd been lucky to escape his grip alive.

Afterwards, her sister Maggie had wanted her to stay with Lorne and the others, even take up residence in the between-worlds—a concept she was still wrapping her mind around. But Linny had refused. What had happened to her had been terrifying. It was nice seeing Maggie happy with her Marquis, but Linny wasn't going anywhere near the Sorceress or any of her pals.

This job as a ghost walker had been a way to

exorcise the past, and so far it was working. With all these 'believers' around her she no longer felt like such a freak.

The tour went smoothly, her commentary second nature to her now. She always kept the best for last. The house of an evil and depraved Baron who kept his serving girls prisoner and had his dastardly way with them, before murdering them and disposing of their bodies in a local graveyard. The place had an atmosphere about it, and even the doubters were on edge by the time she'd finished.

"Ms McNab?" The American girl was tugging her sleeve. "Is that…? Who *is* that?"

Linny looked up with a smile, expecting to see some homeless person with a bottle in a brown paper bag. It happened sometimes. Or else some joker who had a bet with his friends that he could get the tourists to run.

But it was neither. A man was leaning against the wall of the building, in the shadows of the laneway, almost invisible. There was something about him. He was looking down, hands jammed into the pockets of what appeared to be an old fashioned great coat, and as they approached he lifted his head.

Linny caught her breath.

She knew that scar. That dark watchful gaze. She didn't realize she had stopped moving until he began to walk towards her, using an elegant ebony cane to assist with his leg.

The girl at her side gave a cry and stumbled back. "Are you—are you dead?" she asked, her eyes enormous in the light from the street lamp above them.

Darlington considered the question. "Yes, I suppose I am."

Something rattled in the buildings above, and a bird, awoken from its sleep, screeched loudly.

Several women screamed, and in a panic the entire group turned and fled, the clatter of their departure on the cobbles sounding like heavy rain, fading into the distance. Even the man who had attached himself to her side had gone, leaving Linny to her fate.

She stood and waited, watching him cautiously until he reached her. Her heart gave a hitch, as if she was having a minor heart attack, but she didn't want him to know that. She gave him her best bored look. "What are you doing here, your lordship?" she asked him. "Tired of the between-worlds and hankering for a burger?"

He rested on his cane, his eyes taking her in. There was a moment where she thought she might put her arms about him and kiss his cheek, like an old friend, but it passed. Because they weren't old friends and could never be.

"I'm not a lord," he said, but she thought he said it to give himself time to find an answer that wouldn't send her running after the others. "My title was taken from me."

Linny shrugged. He was being scrupulously honest today—he was dead and he'd been stripped of his title. Was he also going to tell her what he was doing in her hometown?

"I'm not alone," he informed her. "Maggie and Lorne are here. Sutcliffe and Loki as well. We're all staying in Blythswood Square."

Of course they were. Lorne had money, and friends with influence. She thought of the Sorceress and forced down a shudder.

"Well, that's all very nice," she said, "and I will see them when I can, but some of us peasants have to work for a living."

Darlington shook his head. His eyes showed regret, and perhaps disapproval, but it didn't matter what he thought of her. She was doing him and the others a big favour. All the same, she checked out his face, trying to see if he was still the man she dreamt of at night.

She couldn't let herself become involved with him. He was two hundred years old, on a mission she could barely comprehend, while she struggled to cope with life in the present decade.

"He's back." He said the words she'd been dreading. And then, just in case she hadn't got the point added, "Stewart. He's here in Glasgow, pretending to be Simon. There have been sightings."

"Simon? My sister's dead husband? Jesus Christ, you guys really don't let the dead lie, do you?" Linny replied sarcastically, but there was a bitter taste in her mouth. She couldn't do this again. Last time she had worried about her sister, sensing something was wrong, she had gone south to Lincolnshire and nearly died for her trouble.

Linny and Maggie McNab were close, with a psychic link they had never fully understood. But now Maggie had Lorne, and Linny didn't have to lay her life on the line to protect her sister anymore. There were others far better qualified than her.

"We think he's doing it to draw us back into his net."

"So why are you here?" Linny repeated impatiently. "Shouldn't you be running as far and fast as you can in the other direction? Or charging into battle like a damned fool?"

"We're here because we have no option," Darlington replied in a solemn voice. "We have to capture him, and this may be our only chance."

"So you thought you'd just drop in on my ghost walk, scare off my customers, and say hello, did you?"

She turned and walked away but, as she'd known he would, Darlington accompanied her, his cane tapping along with their steps. "Linny, I wish for you to join us," he spoke, slightly breathless, making her feel guilty for forcing him to keep up. "There's safety in numbers."

She shook her head. "Oh no you don't," she said. "There's safety in staying the hell away from you lot. Nicholas, you don't know what it was like when—when …" The words stuck in her throat. She swallowed, and forced a smile. "Fare thee well, my lord. Give my best wishes to Maggie. She knows where to find me."

And with that she hurried off, quickening her pace, knowing he couldn't catch her up.

She didn't turn around but she pictured him

standing in the road watching her go, like a scene out of *Les Misérables*.

But that couldn't be helped, she told herself. The rest of them didn't understand. They had seen what happened to her when the Destroyer took over her body, and they had saved her life and brought her back. She was grateful, she truly was, but they didn't understand.

When the demon had been inside her, she had been... elsewhere. And when she'd come back from that other place something had come along with her.

And it was still here.

Chapter Two

Blythswood Square,
Glasgow

MAGGIE BLINKED AND STRETCHED IN the big bed. This was luxury. But more than that, she was just so glad to be out of the between-worlds and back in the mortal world again. The real world. *Her* world. Even if their being here did mean they were also putting themselves in danger.

Stewart had been spotted, taking Simon's form, and it seemed more than possible that he was trying to reel them in like a fish on a line. And they were willing to be reeled, if it meant they could capture Stewart. That was what the Sorceress wanted from them. From Lorne in particular. That was the only reason she hadn't returned him to the past.

"I might pop into the archaeology department at the university," she said casually. "See if they've got anything I might be able to help with."

Lorne was standing at the window, gazing down at the street and a world that constantly amazed him. He wore a black t-shirt and trousers—he seemed to have taken on the Lestat image now they were out of the between-worlds. She wasn't sure whether she preferred this look, or the Regency gentleman he actually was.

He turned and for a moment he was just a silhouette. Then he moved toward her until she could see his face. He wasn't happy.

"You will not leave my sight," he said. She would never tire of that voice. Pure 18th century English gentleman, even when he was being arrogant and overbearing. "Capeesh?"

Well, almost pure. He seemed to have picked up some new words along the way. The bingeing on Mafia movies hadn't been wasted.

"Lorne," she sighed. "I have to do *something*."

He sat down on the bed beside her. Those ice blue eyes warmed with love, and he reached and rested his hand oh-so-gently on her belly. There was barely any sign yet. Just a slight rounding of her tummy that was easily hidden under loose clothing. But they both knew his baby was inside her, growing, and when he or she was born...

Maggie didn't even want to think about whether Lorne would still be here to play his part. Or whether by then he would have been sent back to his own time, to face the consequences of his reckless actions when he brought the demon—the Destroyer—into this world. And what was she meant to do then? She was sure she could manage as a single mother, a lot of women did, but the truth was she didn't want to. It just seemed so unfair.

She hadn't been on the pill since Simon had died, and Lorne found modern contraceptives fascinating after the thicker sheep skin condoms of his time, to the point of admiring his sheathed cock in the mirror while she waited for him, giggling, on the bed. But things had changed.

"Maggie," he said, bringing her back to their discussion. She blinked, and realised that he'd tracked the passage of thoughts and emotions across her face. "When we decided I would give you a child, you knew I might not be here to see it born."

That was true. They had discussed it in the between-worlds, and she had known, and she'd declared it didn't matter. That if he had to go then she wanted something of him to remain, some small part to go on.

"Not many people have this chance," she'd said. "They don't know when they will die, and they can't turn back time and make new decisions. We have that chance."

He had been uncertain.

"Maybe you don't want a child," she'd said, wondering if it was that simple for him. "If so then I understand."

His response had surprised her. "Maggie, you have no idea how much I want a child with you. I want our lives to be lived together, for as long as we have. It's just … the thought of my not being here makes my heart ache unbearably."

She'd reminded him that they didn't know how long it would take to capture Stewart. It might take a year. It might take ten.

That night he had made love to her as if it was his last chance, and by morning Maggie had known in her heart that she had conceived.

Now, in Glasgow, he bent and rested his cheek against her belly. She placed her hand on his dark hair. She had loved her husband Simon, more than she could put into words, but this love had taken her completely unawares, and now it consumed her. She could not think of losing love a second time, she dared not. For her there was only the now.

Next door there was a muffled thump, followed by a woof.

"Aiden does know he isn't supposed to wash Loki in his bathroom?" Maggie said with a frown.

Lorne, officially Charles Escott, the 4th Marquis of Lorne, sat up and glared at the closed door that separated the two apartments. "I have told him."

"Doesn't Nicholas care? He's sharing the bathroom with them. I wouldn't like running a bath only to find it full of dog hairs."

"Darlington seems to have his mind on other matters lately." Lorne glanced sideways at her. "He was out again last night."

"Again?" She sat up properly now, swinging her feet to the floor. The nausea had passed, or at least receded enough for her to think about getting dressed and starting her day.

"What does he do all night in Glasgow? Not that there isn't plenty to do, mind, but I'm not sure the Nicholas Darlington I know is the sort to prop up a bar and drown his sorrows. Maybe he's into kara-oke?" In the days of the Hellfire Club the three men had all drunk themselves silly but over the two hundred years they had been asleep they had changed.

Lorne stood and checked his wristwatch. It was vintage and when Maggie had bought it for him he was gratifyingly delighted. "I did happen to notice a pamphlet on the table in their room," he said. "It was an advertisement for something called 'ghost tours' around the older parts of the city."

Maggie stared at him. "Ghost tours? Somehow, I find that deeply disturbing."

Lorne's serious face cracked into a smile. She loved the way she could make him smile, and sometimes even laugh.

"So did I. I asked Sutcliffe about it when Dar-lington wasn't there."

"What did Aiden say?"

"That Darlington had brought it home with him. Sutcliffe thought that perhaps your sister was involved."

"Linny?" Maggie began to throw on some clothes. "Not sure why she'd be involved in that. I'll go and see her while I'm out. I can ask her what's going on."

"She can come here."

Maggie looked at him over her shoulder. "You know she won't, Lorne. She doesn't want to have anything to do with you or me. With any of us. That night after you saved her? She hasn't spoken about it, she never speaks about it. But something happened and she hasn't been the same since."

She tugged on a fuchsia coloured sweater, releasing her dark, curling mop of hair, while Lorne watched [with flattering attention]. Maggie fumbled with the button on her jeans, realising they were getting tight. She sat down to pull on her boots and zip them up.

"We can only imagine what she saw, or where she went during that time the Destroyer inhabited her body."

"When the Sorceress placed you in the barrow, did you see anything?"

"No. I was asleep, but I was in my own body, Maggie. It may have been different for Linny."

Maggie stared up at him from the bed. After a grim childhood, she and her sister remained close and this current state of affairs between them felt wrong. Linny should be here, part of their team. The worst of it was that they didn't know what Stewart was planning, and until they did no one was safe. She worried about Linny out there on her own.

"I'll talk to her," she said, standing up. "I know where she is. I looked her up."

"Looked her up?" he repeated.

Maggie picked up her smartphone and held it aloft, reminding him how difficult it was for anyone in this modern world to truly disappear.

"I should tell Sutcliffe where we're going." Lorne automatically assumed he was accompanying her. Because of course he did. He moved to the door that led into the neighbouring apartment. When he opened it, Sutcliffe was standing in the middle of the room. Naked.

Maggie spun around, face flaming, but Lorne took no notice. She had once had the opportunity to see echoes of Lorne and his friends as the men they were before, during their Hellfire Club days. She knew they had performed many intimate acts in each other's company, but she preferred not to remember.

She hadn't liked Lorne and his two friends as they'd been back then. But then, she had the impression they hadn't liked themselves much, either. She much preferred the men they were now.

She picked up her backpack and slung it over her shoulder. It felt more important than ever to find her sister and speak with her. To understand what was going on in her head.

Linny had always been the one to worry about her. She was there through all of Maggie's difficulties, as well as her triumphs. Maggie had been a young prodigy when she reached university—excelling academically, but emotionally she had struggled. Then she'd married her professor, Simon, and they had embarked on what they had hoped would be a long and happy marriage. It hadn't turned out that way. Simon had died far too young. Without Linny, Maggie wouldn't have been able to cope. Now, it was time for Maggie to do the worrying.

She had reached the door into the street when Lorne caught up with her, slipping his arm about her waist and drawing her close. She looked to him and raised her eyebrows.

"You really don't need to come. I'm fine."

His expression suggested otherwise. "Stewart is here in Glasgow," he reminded her. "That makes it very far from fine, Maggie. No arguing. I'm coming with you."

Chapter Three

NICHOLAS DARLINGTON SWALLOWED THE APPALLING swill that passed for coffee in this world. He could have complained, thrown it back into the face of the boy who'd handed it to him, knowing that in the past his social status would have protected him from retribution. But this modern world was different. Questions would be asked, accusations made, and he might be strong-armed out of the cafe. He didn't want to leave because it was right opposite the office where Linny was working.

Glaswegian Ghost Tours.

That was what the sign over the door said, in the kind of gothic lettering that was meant to send chills down the spine. If that didn't work then the silhouette of a howling ghost in a shroud made their intentions perfectly clear.

Linny's habit was to come in after noon. Today she was late, but perhaps that was his fault. His appearance in the laneway last night had alarmed her and she may not have slept well. He only hoped she had not decided to run off to some other part of the country just to escape him. Not that he thought she would. Linny McNab was made of sterner stuff.

At that moment she appeared further down the street, making her way slowly toward her work-place. Her blonde hair was loose, strands of it tangled by the cold wind. Her head was bent for-ward and her hands dug deep into the pockets of her black coat. She wore high heeled boots and tight trousers, and she was the most beautiful thing he had seen since ... well, since last night.

For a moment he was dizzy, as he remembered the first time he'd met her at Maggie's cottage. She'd turned up out of nowhere, stamped her undeniable presence on the moment, and demanded to know who they were.

He couldn't forget her. Spending the past few months confined in the between-worlds had been agony for him. All he'd wanted to do was find her and see if that incredible spark he had felt between them had been more than a figment of his imag-ination. Last night when he'd walked out of the shadows, he'd been certain that what he'd seen in her face, in her eyes, was relief. Relief and joy that he had come to her at last. Then she'd wiped those emotions away and left him with nothing but doubt again.

Linny had just about reached the office when a man abruptly moved away from the wall he had been leaning against and stepped in front of her. Nicholas had paid him no heed, taking him for just another resident, but now he perceived a possible threat. He stood up, spilling his coffee on the table. The boy behind the counter turned to him with startled eyes, but Nicholas was already on his way out the door.

He could tell the man wasn't Stewart, but that relief was short lived when he remembered that Stewart could have changed into another form. He quickened his pace across the uneven road, barely noticing the pain in his lame leg.

The closer he came to them, the clearer he could hear Linny's voice. She was angry and didn't bother to hide it.

"You want *what*?" she demanded. "Go to hell Keith, that's what I say. Go right to hell. And trust me, I know *exactly* what hell is like!"

Then, as if she had sensed him, her gaze moved past the shaggy head of the man in front of her and found Darlington. For a moment she seemed at a loss for words, but not for long. Her eyes narrowed.

"You again? I don't need your help," she told him bluntly. "I can handle my ex-husband perfectly well on my own."

"Of course you can," Nicholas said with quiet satisfaction. Linny was never at a loss when it came to expressing her feelings. "I was just watching. I like to watch."

Keith turned around. His face was unshaven and he had a number of metal objects inserted into it—one through his eyebrow, another in his nose and more in his ear. As for his clothing, that looked crumpled, as if he had just got up out of bed, and the striped article of clothing that Nicholas had recently learned was called a football jersey, had a stain on the front. It was obvious that he was not happy with the situation.

Linny had continued to stare past her ex-husband in Nicholas's direction. She gave a throaty laugh. "Some would call what you're doing stalking," she said. Before he could answer she shot Keith a contemptuous look. "Now, move aside. I have to get to work."

"You can't walk away," Keith whined. "I want to talk to you."

"There's nothing left to say. I made a mistake. I've moved on."

"You owe me money and I want it." Keith reached for her arm, but she evaded him and gave him a shove that made him stumble to one side. He came into her space again, and this time tried to grab her around the waist.

A moment later he was sprawled on the ground.

Startled, Linny looked at Nicholas rubbing his fist, and then down at her ex-husband. She smiled. "Oops."

That smile heated up his blood and brought to life that part of him which had not had any engagements in a very long time.

Keith scrambled to his feet and began to spit out his anger in a low and furious voice. "Fuck you, Linny! You'll regret this. Both of you!"

They stood and watched him stumble away down the hill.

"I could have handled him on my own," Linny

said at last. "There was no need for you to come to my rescue."

"Even if it gave me great pleasure to do so?" he asked curiously.

She bit her lip, holding back a grin. "Even then." Her dark eyes slid over him as if she had noticed his outfit for the first time. He wore the same clothes as last night, for the simple reason that he hadn't gone back to the apartment and he hadn't been to bed. He supposed his lack of sleep was obvious, although the encounter with Keith had given his spirits quite a lift.

"Come away in," Linny said with a sigh. "Then at least I can put a plaster on your wee cut."

Nicholas looked down at his hand. He hadn't realised that he had caught his fist on one of those metal decorations. The cut was nothing. He'd experienced a great deal worse—one only had to look at the scar that ran down his cheek, and then there was the mess made of his leg. Yes, the *wee* cut was nothing, but Linny had offered and his acquiescence gained him entry into her building, and more time with her.

As he followed her inside it felt like a victory, but he was quick to push down his sense of triumph. He'd always known instinctively what to say to women to insinuate himself into their good graces. But Linny was different. She was a puzzle in so many ways.

When she had arrived at her sister's cottage in Lincolnshire he had sensed an immediate connection between Linny and himself. But then Stewart had sent his demon out to kill her. Lorne had brought her back to life, but soon afterwards she'd pulled away, both physically and emotionally. While he was locked up in the between-worlds, his need to see her had been a constant ache within him.

Now he'd found her again, and though his life was full of uncertainty, of one thing he was sure. He wasn't about to let her go so easily this time.

———◆———

Linny was already stripping off her coat as she moved through the crowded office area to the little room that she called her own. A couple of employees were already there, eyes widening when they noticed her companion, but she didn't stop to explain. Once she and Darlington were inside her sanctuary, she firmly closed her door and leaned back against it and looked at him.

Despite his attractive looks, Nicholas Darlington had the aura of a desperate and dangerous man, and that made him seriously hot in her eyes. When he'd dealt with Keith … well, as she'd said, she could have handled it herself, but seeing him play the hero was really very impressive. She had half-expected him to challenge her ex-husband to a duel and run him through with a sword.

God, was that image sexy or what? But as much as she'd love to be rid of her troublesome mistake, she was pretty sure that Keith dead would be even more of a problem than Keith alive. Her taste in men had never been great, something she needed to remember before she flung herself into the arms of her rescuer.

"What are you doing here?" she asked, hanging her coat and scarf on the rack.

Nicholas leaned back against her desk, one leg stretched out in front of him. He had been doing some staring of his own, examining the advertising posters on the walls, which were all to do with the company's ghost tours, complete with spooky colours and promises to scare you witless. In a good way, naturally.

She reminded herself that he had certainly scared her punters witless last night. It had been slightly awkward when she'd tried to explain the situation to her boss, although he'd taken it better than she'd expected. They'd already paid, he had reminded her, and part of their remit was to see a ghost. Her job was safe. Unless any of them had been in this morning, demanding their money back…

"I was in the neighbourhood, as you say." Nicholas seemed to think he was being clever, and looked surprised when she chuckled in response.

"Where did you hear that? On television? You're a terrible liar, do you know that? You followed me here." Strangely, after his initial look of surprise he appeared pleased by her accusation. As if being a bad liar was somehow a badge of honour. He had probably been accused of far worse.

A knock on the door interrupted whatever he had been about to say. Her boss poked his head inside before she could say she was busy.

"Linny, I… " He noticed Darlington and his eyes

widened. "Is this the…?"

Linny forced a smile. "Yes, this is my 'ghost.' I'm sorry, Davey. Has someone asked for a refund? It was a joke. I'll pay you back."

But her boss was shaking his head. "No one has asked for a refund. Most of them were thrilled … when they finally stopped running. A genuine ghost! Well, as far as they were concerned. We've double the bookings for tonight."

Linny stared at him. "*Double*? You're joking?"

"Word gets around."

Davey was a little too interested in Darlington, however, and she tried not to give in to her urge to step in front of her Regency gentleman, and shield him from her boss. She reminded herself that Davey couldn't possibly know that the character he was so intrigued by was something straight out of a history novel.

"He really is perfect for the part. Where did you find him? I hope this isn't an advertisement for a new brand of whisky. He's not going to whip a bottle out of his coat and start spruiking its superior qualities, is he?"

He was teasing but Nicholas didn't know that. He straightened up, coming to her aid instantly. "There was no deception involved, sir," he said, sounding exactly like what he was—an anachronism. "Linny was not at fault."

Davey ogled him a moment, then gave a shout of laughter and clapped his hands. "Perfect," he said. "Absolutely perfect. Come on, McNab, tell me. Where you found him."

Linny pulled a face. "He found me."

"Well if you're looking for a job, you've found one. Do exactly what you did last night. People will be expecting a rerun. He's not a ghost, and we don't want to be accused of deception, so I'll make that clear. It's all part of the fun."

"Davey, I really don't think…" Linny began doubtfully.

"Trust me, it'll be fine." He gave her a thumbs up and then he was gone, the door closed behind him.

Nicholas met her eyes, looking bewildered, and Linny decided to explain. "He wants you to pretend to be a ghost. At least for one more night. I can't believe that people will still pay to see you, not once word gets around that you're just a man. Well … you know what I mean." She shrugged. "Anyway, tonight my boss thinks he's going to make a killing. A lot of money, that is," she quickly corrected herself.

After a moment, when he said nothing, she added, "You can say no. You don't have to do it."

He smiled. "Why should I say no? All I'm currently doing is sitting in our hotel, listening to Lorne and Maggie playing cupid next door, or watching Sutcliffe and Loki eat their way through the menu. It was bad enough in the between-worlds when we were all locked in there together, like virgins at a—"

He stopped, as if he was concerned for her delicate sensibilities, and now it was she who bit back a smile.

"I had hoped when we left the Sorceress's domain

that we would be more proactive in this burdensome matter. Not just twiddling our thumbs and expecting Stewart to find us."

Linny knew the story of the Hellfire Club. The basics, at any rate. Three nobles had unleashed an evil upon the world long ago, and as punishment had been sent to sleep by someone known only as the Sorceress. Then they were awoken two hundred years later, when the Destroyer they'd set loose came back to life.

That had been her sister's fault, after a fashion. Maggie had arrived to supervise an archaeological dig in the grounds of Blackfriars Abbey, and had accidentally set things in motion. The person behind it all, however, was a man named Stewart, though he was no longer a man. What he was exactly was a mystery to her still.

Linny had travelled to the Abbey, sensing Maggie was in danger, only to have her body taken over by the Destroyer. They had feared she was dead but managed to bring her back to life again. All should have been well, and even Maggie believed her sister had returned without repercussions.

Except there had been repercussions. And that was something she didn't want to discuss with Nicholas Darlington, or anyone else for that matter.

As for Lorne and Maggie shagging in the room next door… she sympathised. It must be awkward for the other two men. But she'd seen the way her sister and Lorne looked at each other. They were in love—crazy turbo charged kind of love—and once the bedroom door was closed they were hardly going to be watching Netflix.

Linny couldn't complain, considering all the times she had advised her sister to get laid! Although she admitted to herself that when she'd made the suggestion, it hadn't been a 'forever' man she had been thinking of. With Maggie's husband Simon dead not quite two years, the last thing Maggie needed was to launch herself into another major relationship. She could have found some nice nerdy bloke who made her smile and pushed her buttons, but wouldn't be too worried when Maggie finally moved on. Instead, she had set her sights on an 18th century Marquis who sent most of the female population into a state of heart pounding, craziness just by showing up.

But the Marquis of Lorne only had eyes for Maggie. Lucky for him, otherwise Linny would have sent him back underground herself.

Linny brought herself back to the present. "So, you'll do it?" She made her voice brisk. "You'll play the ghost again tonight?"

"Yes," he said with a curt nod.

She shook her head. "I don't know what this is going to lead to, except trouble, but frankly I don't care. I never intended to make this job my vocation."

"And what, exactly, is your vocation?" he asked.

She began to tell him, but then changed her mind. Nicholas Darlington knew enough about her already, and telling him another one of her secrets would only ramp up their level of intimacy.

She didn't need the added complication. The less he knew the better. "I want to travel," she said instead. "I'm saving up for a holiday in the sun."

"I lived in Italy for a time," he said. His eyes were on her face. He was the only man she knew who was able to give her his complete and utter attention without it seeming creepy. He didn't seem to be distracted at all, just focussed. She wasn't sure that focus was entirely appropriate, but it was certainly flattering.

"Did you like it? Italy?"

"My family sent me. They hoped it would make me a better man. Or perhaps they simply hoped I would catch a fever and die."

She tried not to be shocked at his matter of fact tone. He was obviously speaking the truth, or at least the truth as he perceived it. "Didn't you get on, you and your family?" she asked. She was curious despite the warning she had just given herself about levels of intimacy.

"I wasn't a nice man in those days." He admitted this in a resigned way as if it was a necessary truth to unburden.

"So they were right to send you away?" She knew she was probing, but she couldn't seem to stop.

He shrugged, which was hardly an answer.

Linny tapped her foot. She could ask for more, but she told herself she wouldn't. "Well, much as I'd like to stay here and chat with you, your lordship, I have work to do. How about we meet up here tonight, about seven? That's when my ghost tour starts."

"I know."

"Oh, right, the whole stalking thing. Of course you know."

He raised a single eyebrow and for a moment she was completely lost. Linny had always had a thing about men who could do that. So sexy, especially when combined with that scar and his bad boy persona.

She realised he'd been speaking and she'd missed most of it. "What did you say?"

He patiently repeated himself, apparently clueless as to her emotional state. "I said: Don't you want me to step out of the laneway, like before? If I meet you here they'll all see me. Don't you want to save the best for last?"

"Of course they will," she replied, with a touch of irritation at her own lack of attention. "You're right. The lane would be better."

"I'll make sure I'm waiting in the same place," he reassured her. "Am I all right dressed like this?"

She looked him up and down. Despite him wearing modern clothes, he'd been able to recreate his past remarkably well. Tight fitting trousers similar to old-fashioned breeches, a loose shirt, rather like something a romantic poet might wear, and that big, caped coat, which she remembered was called a 'great coat'. His brown, shoulder length hair was neatly tied back with a ribbon, and with the addition of his ebony walking stick, this man really couldn't have fitted the part of 'ghost' better if he had auditioned.

"Linny?"

She hadn't answered him because her mouth was suddenly dry with a combination of lust and longing.

"No," she said. "You're perfect just as you are."

He smiled as if it was a compliment, which it was. "Until tonight then," he said.

Linny waited until he was gone before she sank down into her chair with a groan. What was she going to do? Davey had made it impossible for her to send Nicholas away, but even without his intervention she doubted that she would have been able to do that.

As if her life wasn't complicated enough, she had to fancy a 200 year old English gentleman on a mission to destroy evil. And she was starting to worry that it wasn't just 'fancying' him that was the problem. No, not just a one night stand. She had a feeling one night with Nicholas Darlington would never be enough.

Maybe I could tell him the truth? I could tell him what is happening to me?

But there was no point. She needed to stay away from the others and particularly from Maggie. She and Maggie had always had a sixth sense about each other. Her sister's recent romance with Lorne seemed to have blunted it, or perhaps it was her being in the between-worlds, but Linny knew in her heart that Maggie was no longer safe, and she refused to bring down more trouble on her sister's head.

She closed her eyes, relaxing until she was almost

dozing away. Then, just for an instant, she quickly opened them again. A quick sweep of the room failed to find *it*, but that didn't mean it wasn't there. Watching her and waiting.

She relaxed again. Linny was tired, so tired. Since her possession that night at Maggie's cottage in Lincolnshire, her sleeping patterns had been all over the place, and when she did sleep there were nightmares. Everything had been so much worse more recently, now she knew what was lurking beyond that thin veil of slumber. *It* seemed as good a word as any. And if she actually allowed herself to sink into that longed for oblivion, the sleep her body was crying out for so desperately, then it would come through the curtain between its world and hers. She knew it could do that, she'd seen it with her own eyes.

And every time it came through it crept closer to her sleeping, vulnerable self. And Linny didn't think, she really didn't, that it had anything good in mind for her.

Chapter Four

LINNY'S HOUSE WAS EMPTY. SHE lived in the south of the city, in an area Maggie said was new and much nicer than the tenement in which she and her sister had grown up. To Lorne it appeared small and bland, every house the same as its neighbour, all the way along the street. Not that he said so. Last time he made some comment about the inadequacy of a dwelling, Maggie had lectured him on his elitist attitude.

As he had explained to her, it wasn't his fault he had been born a marquis with an abbey and a fortune, and far too much time on his hands. The last bit had made her smile.

Lorne stood outside the house, staring at the blank windows while Maggie went through the side gate to check the rear entrance.

He tried not to glance behind him. It wasn't that he expected to see Stewart standing there waiting for him, but the American was constantly on his mind. So much depended on his capture. Until that time, Lorne's fate hung in the balance. He would remain here with Maggie and his unborn child only as long as it took to do as the Sorceress commanded, and after that … he must return to his time and complete his penance. Tempted as he sometimes was to run away from the whole situation his better self would never allow it, and nor would the Sorceress.

Maggie reappeared, a frown on her face. "She's not home. I don't understand it. I texted to say we'd be here." She tucked a curl of hair behind her ear and considered the problem.

She was wearing a scarlet coat and jeans that clung to her slim hips and long legs, and he was distracted long enough for her to notice.

"What do you think, Lorne?"

"I could break down the front door," Lorne suggested half-heartedly. "The wood appears flimsy enough."

"Thank you for the offer, though I doubt my sister would appreciate it."

At times like this, Lorne wasn't sure Linny appreciated anything whatsoever about him. The sisters were very close, and if Linny didn't consider him good enough to lick Maggie's boots then he couldn't help but agree with her. Becoming a better man was a constant battle, but he was determined never to allow the bad habits of two centuries past to raise their ugly heads. He had been remoulded into someone Maggie loved. That was reason enough not to backslide.

Lorne finally gave in and looked over his shoulder. No Stewart, thank the gods. The street was empty apart from Maggie's hire car. What had he expected? His enemy wasn't going to make this easy for him. He and his friends would have to risk their lives once more if they were going to find redemption and undo what they'd done.

He turned back to find Maggie looking under pot plants. When he asked her why, she said her sister might have left a spare door key. "There's something wrong, Lorne," she said. "I can feel it. There's been something wrong ever since her body was taken over by the Destroyer. I know you saved her life, but…" She straightened up. "But what if I was distracted and didn't pay enough attention to what was going on?"

"Distracted?" he repeated with note of mockery.

She came over and slipped her hand into his. "Distracted in a good way. I just wish she would talk to me. She can be so stubborn."

"And you're not?"

She sighed. "Not like her. Lorne, this is something I have to do. I want to do. You don't have to come with me. In fact—"

"If you insist on going to the university and putting yourself in danger, then I am coming with you," he said. Lorne knew her well enough by now to realize he had only two choices. Tie her up and leave her in their room or come with her. He had chosen the latter. He was, after all, supposed to be a better man.

"Thank you." Her voice softened. "I know you think I'm risking myself and the baby, but Simon has been seen at the university. In his old rooms."

"Maggie, you know it's not Simon. Stewart duped you before."

"I know." She nodded and he could see how difficult she found this. "But if he's insisting on keeping Simon's form, it's for a reason. And it might not have to do with me. Lorne, I want to talk to people, people who knew Simon. Perhaps it will help us to find Stewart."

He put his arms around her and she leaned into him. The situation was a strain on them both, but more so for her. And always at the back of their minds was the knowledge that someday he would be sent back to the past, and it would be Maggie who would stay and bring up their child.

They had argued about the matter before. Maggie wanted to go back with him when the time came and he'd said no, that it was too dangerous. His fate was most likely to be lynched by an angry mob and what would happen to her then? If he did as the Sorceress asked, if he returned Stewart to her, then he would beg her to allow him to stay here in the mortal world, with Maggie. Whether the Sorceress would grant his wish or refuse it was anyone's guess. There was no use trying to read the mind of the witch. All he could do was obey to the best of his ability, to undo the damage that he had done, and spend what precious time he could with the woman he loved.

"I will do all in my power." He rested his cheek against hers, taking in the feel and scent of her. "*All* in my power, Maggie, to stay here with you."

She turned her face to kiss him. "I know you

will," she whispered. "I know."

His mouth covered hers, their kisses full of love and passion and fear of loss. Lorne wondered if his selfish longing for a child with her had been wrong. Another misstep in a long life full of them. If he had once again allowed his baser instincts to stop him from being the better man.

———◆———

The university buildings were very old. Simon had been a resident here for quite some time before he became ill. Maggie loved this place, though she suspected Lorne found it oppressive, reminding him of the misery he had endured at the boarding school of his youth. Unlike Maggie, he was no scholar. But he put on a brave face for her and she was grateful for that. As they walked along the echoing corridors, she reminded herself what she already knew: Simon, her husband, was gone. Whatever was out there masquerading as him, it was not Simon, and that made her angry.

Lorne watched her restless movements. "Maggie. Enough."

"I wish he would face us," she said, and glared at the empty air. She was angry that Stewart was using Simon like this. Ever since he was a child, the bastard son of Nanny Noakes had hated Lorne with a passion that knew no bounds. He had become a suffocating darkness, an evil force, and he would do anything, destroy anything, to take his revenge.

"If he does then I am prepared," Lorne said, patting his shirt pocket.

"You have the ring?"

"Always."

She met his eyes, aware of the gravity in them. The ring had been given to Lorne by the Sorceress and was to be placed on Stewart's finger. Once that was done he would be under the witch's control and no longer a threat to the world. Or the Hellfire Club.

Maggie's mobile pinged. She dragged it out of her pocket.

"Aiden," she said for Lorne's benefit, and held it so that he could read the message. His friend's attempts at texting always lifted her spirits.

Where r u?

She smiled, pleased he had mastered the basics of time efficiency.

At the university. Why?

Darlington isn't back. Worried. Loki's hungry.

Maggie sighed. "What is it with Nicholas going off all the time? Do you know where he is?"

Lorne shrugged. "We haven't really discussed the matter." He glanced at her as if he'd had a sudden thought and wasn't sure whether to share it. "He was very taken with your sister, as I recall."

Nicholas and Linny? She tried to imagine it. Her strong willed, no nonsense sister, and Nicholas Darlington, scarred on the outside and no doubt inside too.

Her phone pinged again.

"Sutcliffe?" Lorne handed her a takeaway cup of coffee he had acquired from somewhere. He'd probably simply been standing in the right place at the right time, Maggie told herself. Lorne had the devil's own luck most of the time.

She glanced down at her new message. "Yep. I suppose we should go back to the hotel. Aiden says Nicholas was out all night."

Lorne turned to set down his coffee and Maggie froze. Because right before her, where the stairs descended in a sweep from the upper floor, was her dead husband.

Despite all she knew about Stewart and his deceptions, she struggled to believe this was not the man she had married. It looked like him, it moved like him. *Simon* was walking down those stairs. He was looking at his feet, but when he reached the last step he lifted his head and paused, like an actor making the most of a dramatic moment.

Maggie's throat closed over. Their eyes met and her heart told her this *must* be Simon. He gave her the sort of smile he used when they were sharing something intimate, something personal. And then, before she could react, he stepped off the staircase and moved swiftly down a corridor, away from her.

Now, with his gaze no longer on her, she could think clearly again. Maggie set off at a run after him.

"Lorne!" she shouted. "Quickly! He's down here."

Simon was at the end of the corridor now. How could he move so quickly? She was never going to catch him, and maybe that was the point. Stewart was teasing them, playing his creepy, cruel games.

Maybe he wasn't ready to confront them yet. As she knew from their past encounters, the American had his own black-hearted agenda where Lorne was concerned.

Maggie reached the end of the corridor, which broke into a T intersection, with longer corridors running at right angles across it. Stewart could have gone either way, but he was nowhere in sight. In front of her was a small window which overlooked a quadrangle. She moved to look out. Just for a moment she thought she saw Stewart's back, and then he was gone.

"Maggie?" Lorne finally caught up to her.

"I saw him." Her voice was barely audible. "Simon … Stewart. It was him."

She could see he believed her. He knew her, and Stewart, too well to think she was mistaken.

"He wanted you to see him," he said, mirroring her own thoughts.

"I think so, yes. It was magic again. He was moving far too quickly to be a real, mortal man. I was never meant to catch up to him."

Lorne frowned. "More games." He reached over and tucked a dark curl behind her ear. "You're upset."

"Yes." She sighed. "I hate seeing Simon like this. Even though I know it's not him, it feels so wrong. Alive or dead, Simon doesn't deserve to be used in this way. Like some kind of puppet."

"Stewart knows how to bring us into his reach. He knows you are vulnerable where your late husband is concerned. Don't be taken in by him,

Maggie."

His pale eyes were slightly anxious. Maggie remembered the last time Stewart fooled her into thinking he was her late husband, sending her back in time to 1808, when the Hellfire Club was in full swing. She still had nightmares about what she saw.

"No, I won't be taken in by him again," she reassured Lorne. "On the other hand, he must want us here. He wants us in Glasgow, for now at any rate. What do you think he has planned?"

Lorne's handsome face turned serious. "Nothing good. We must be ready for anything, Maggie. I won't underestimate him again, you can be sure of that."

Chapter Five

L INNY LED HER GLASWEGIAN GHOST
Tours group through the old, narrow streets of
her home town. There were certainly a lot more
punters tonight, but she didn't believe they were
entirely serious when it came to the 'ghost' sighting
her boss had promised them. From the giggles and
nudges they exchanged as she waited for everyone
to arrive, she suspected they were in party mode.

As long as they didn't burst out laughing when
they saw Nicholas, she thought. Although she
couldn't imagine anyone in their right mind doing
that. Nicholas Darlington had a presence. When he
turned his attention on you it was nearly impossible to think rationally, let alone look away.

Her skin prickled, and an ache started low in her
belly.

Stop it. Bloody hormones. There was absolutely
no time for this sort of behaviour, she informed
herself in the sort of sharp and reproving voice
she'd used on her sister when they were small and
she refused to do her homework. But unlike Mag-

gie all those years ago, Linny wasn't listening.

She hadn't had a man in her bedroom, in her *life*, since before she'd driven all the way down to Blackfriars Abbey, and it was unlikely there would be one in the near future. Maybe never again, she thought bleakly. She'd stripped everything down to the bare minimum. She went to work and ate meals that required little preparation, mostly take-out. She conserved her energy and dragged herself through each day, barely clinging to a world she wasn't sure she was still a part of. Sex should be unimportant when she was simply trying to survive.

But it wasn't.

Acknowledging that her life was in danger somehow made sex even *more* important. It was as if her libido, on hiatus, had lifted its head when Nicholas Darlington showed up back in her life, given a blink, and then a wide smile of anticipation.

Now that libido was demanding she satisfy it.

Linny was determined that wasn't going to happen, and although there were times when she wondered why she didn't just give in and enjoy what might be her last days on earth, she knew the real reason why. There was more to what she was feeling for Nicholas than the need for sex. The situation was messy and complicated, and contained the sort of emotions she hadn't gone near since she made the mistake of marrying Keith.

She was pulled out of her thoughts when a profile in the group in front of her caught her eye for a moment, only to vanish again as someone else pushed in front. Linny blinked, certain she recognised that face. Before she could compel her tired brain to drag the memory out, a tall man with a Londoner's accent claimed her attention, asking a question about the history of the city. By the time she had finished with him, she had forgotten about the familiar face.

It was time now for her scripted tour talk. Calling for silence, she made a start.

"This building you see in front of us was once the home of the Duke of Rattray, who threw his wife from the roof." She did her best to curdle their blood with horror, but as she'd noted none of them were in a blood curdling mood. They listened politely, and it wasn't until they were about to move on that the real trouble began.

"Surely if this Duke did the things you say he did he would have been torn apart by the mob?"

The aristocratic male voice was instantly recognisable. Linny turned her head, searching through the crowd, and spotted Maggie's Marquis.

"What are you doing here?" she asked Lorne rudely, making the sort of stern face that usually saw off the hecklers.

He smiled, unmoved. "Why, I've come to see the ghost," he said.

Another head loomed up above the others, and Sutcliffe grinned at her. "Can't wait," he announced. "I've heard this spectre is spectacular."

Linny tried not to groan. Why hadn't she noticed those two before now? Was it one of their faces she had thought she recognized as they were setting out? She didn't think so. If Lorne or Sutcliffe had been in the crowd then she wouldn't have had to look twice.

Linny moved toward the two men and the group parted for her. Interested faces were turned their way, no doubt assuming this was part of the script. She glared from Lorne to Sutcliffe and back again, but they were unmoved. "You're spoiling things," she hissed. "Go away."

Lorne looked at Sutcliffe and affected surprise. "You paid, didn't you, Aiden?"

"Of course I did. Didn't you?"

"Most definitely."

Aware of the shuffling behind her and impatient murmurs, Linny had no option but to back down. "Just don't cause any trouble," she warned them, then spun on her heel and returned to the head of the group.

She'd half expected to see her sister somewhere, but there was no sign of Maggie. Well, at least she would be spared that! She tried not to imagine the look on Maggie's face when she found out how Linny was earning her living. The frowns and worried glances and the questions that would be asked of her—questions she didn't know how to answer.

"Come on everyone, this way!" She waved them on. The rest of the tour was uneventful, but she suspected that would change when Nicholas appeared. When they reached their final stop and were obediently quiet and attentive, she lowered her voice in an attempt to make this more intimate, although there were far too many of them for her efforts to be entirely successful.

"You see that wee alley up there? Well, there's a ghost been seen recently. Probably the wraith of a Baron who murdered his serving wenches and then hid their bodies. It's said that he's still hunt-ing for victims, and he lurks in the shadows, and sometimes follows those who pass by. They don't know he's there until they hear the tap, tap, tap of his walking cane behind them."

"Sounds like a most unpleasant chap." Sutcliffe spoke in what he probably thought was a whisper.

"A brute, I'd say," Lorne added.

These two wouldn't know how to be 'subtle' if their lives depended on it.

Above them the street lamp suddenly flickered before it blinked out, and plunged them into, if not pitch black, then a dark and gloomy grey. There were some cries from her group, even a muffled scream. That was good, Linny thought. Perhaps all of their earlier jokes and laughter had been to disguise their fear—they certainly weren't joking now. In fact, they seemed to have shuffled closer together, as if for safety. One of them even trod on the toe of Linny's boot.

"There he is!" Someone cried out in an excited voice.

Everyone followed the pointing finger. Linny held her breath. *Show time.*

Darlington left the shadows at the entrance to the laneway and took a step toward them. His cane tapped on the cobbles, his great coat hung heavy about him. Silence. The group watched, shuffling nervously, but no one ran. Perhaps they wouldn't tonight.

"Good evening," his voice was soft and menacing. Perhaps a bit too theatrical, but convincing.

"Is it…?" Lorne began.

"Can it be…?" Sutcliffe played along.

"*The Baron's ghost!*" They roared out together.

Everyone turned and ran.

Linny sighed as she stood alone and waited for the clatter of fleeing tourists to fade once again into silence.

"Like virgins at a rogering ball." Nicholas made his way to her side. He looked pleased with himself, although not so pleased to see his two friends. "How did you find me?" he asked them. Then, to Linny, "Did you tell them?"

Lorne spoke up. "Maggie found out where Linny was working from some reptile called Keith. When we made our way to the tour office, we were told we could see a genuine 'ghost'." He smirked. "Then they described him."

Sutcliffe chuckled. "Ironic, isn't it? A ghost taking paid employment to play a ghost."

Darlington snorted, unamused. "At least I am doing something. All you two do is sit around and wait for life to happen. I'm out living it."

The two men looked annoyed by that comment, but Linny wasn't about to let this turn into an argument. "As much as I'd like to stay and chat," she said, raising her voice, "I'd better go and find my customers. Make sure none get lost."

"Should I come too?" Nicholas asked.

She couldn't help but smile. "Maybe not a good idea, my lord. They'll just stampede again, and I'll never catch up with them."

"We'll take him home with us," Sutcliffe said. "Come on, Nicholas. Loki is missing you."

"Loki only cares about you," Nicholas muttered. "And food."

Sutcliffe took his arm in a friendly gesture, but Linny thought it more likely he was worried about his friend's balance on the uneven cobbles.

"Goodbye," she called after them. Nicholas raised his arm without turning around.

She made her way toward the nearest pub, expecting to find most of her customers there, only to find Lorne blocking her path. She'd forgotten about the Marquis. He stepped aside and began to walk beside her. She sensed he wasn't just being a gentleman, but had something important to say to her.

She was sure Lorne was a very nice man. He had to be, or Maggie wouldn't be so crazy about him. And yet he made her uncomfortable for reasons she didn't quite understand. Maybe because he was so good looking, so appealing. Men like that, in her experience, were not to be trusted, and it came as a relief that she didn't feel attracted to him the way she did Darlington. There was something else, though. She didn't like to admit it to herself, and she certainly wasn't going to admit it to Maggie. Her sister trusted Lorne to take care of her, while Linny didn't.

For a time they walked together in silence, the

chilly night enveloping them.

"Maggie wanted to come tonight," he said at last.

"I'm glad she didn't."

More silence. She wondered if he was ever going to speak again, and just as they were in sight of the pub's windows, he did.

"You need to come and see her."

She stopped and put a hand on her hip. "Why? Because you say so?"

"Because if you don't she'll be here tomorrow night. She knows there's something wrong. She feels it."

Linny eyed him uneasily. "What could be wrong?"

He made an impatient sound that reminded her of Maggie. It was actually rather endearing. As if they had taken on each other's mannerisms without knowing it. "You should trust us, Linny. We can keep you safe."

"No one can keep me safe, pal. I keep myself safe. Always have."

She sounded bitter and resigned. She wanted to take the words back, but it was too late. Lorne stared at the bright lights of the pub where she suspected her tour group were already telling tall tales.

"Maybe we can't keep you safe, but Maggie thinks we can. We need to stay together until we send Stewart back to hell where he belongs."

She shuddered. *Hell.* Was that where she had gone when the Destroyer took her body? It wasn't somewhere she'd add to her bucket list, not voluntarily. Even Stewart didn't deserve to go there. No, scratch that, he did.

"And I might not always be here," Lorne added, and the words seemed forced from him. "Maggie will need you then."

This didn't sound like the Lorne she knew. This sounded like a desperate man who, for the first time in his life, was asking for her help. She should have considered her response more carefully, but her past experiences along with her fears for Maggie's future brought the words spewing out before she could stop them.

"What do you mean you might not always be here? Are you planning on ditching her already? Because if you are, Stewart is going to have to make room in hell for you, you understand?"

His pale eyes narrowed and he shook his head in disgust. "Just go and see her," he said in a cold, hard voice. "Whatever you think of me, she needs you."

She watched him walk away, and Linny wished she could take her words back. She knew about the pact Lorne had made with the Sorceress. To save Maggie's life he had given his life, more or less. It was a heroic thing to do, selfless and brave.

Then why didn't she believe him? Was she … could she be … jealous? More likely she was struggling to believe that a man with a reputation like his was really fit to lick her little sister's boots.

She and Maggie had always been close, more like mother and daughter than sisters. It was all right for Linny to muck up her life, choose the wrong men, make the wrong life choices, but not Maggie. She wasn't allowed to. Until recently, Maggie had stuck to the road map Linny had laid out for her. But the Marquis was a very big detour from that map, and just maybe Linny was finding it difficult to accept this was going to be the happy ever after she envisaged for her sister.

Perhaps, in her secret heart, Linny believed the best thing that could happen was for Lorne to be returned to the past and whatever fate awaited him there as quickly as possible.

She hastened her step and headed into the pub. Yeah, her life was a complete mess, there was no doubting that. And as far as she could see there was no fixing it. But there was *one* thing she could do right, and she didn't need Lorne to boss her into doing it. She could stand by her sister.

Chapter Six

THE NEXT MORNING, LINNY ARRIVED at her sister's swish hotel. She hesitated at the front doors. Through the shiny glass she could see the doorman in his red uniform, giving her a suspicious once over. Maybe he could tell just from looking that she didn't belong here. She'd never belonged in places like this, and she'd never wanted to. The McNabs were common folk, with minds of their own. They made their own way in life in the world. Made their own rules. The fact that Maggie had attached herself to a Marquis, even if he was two hundred years old, seemed like a betrayal of the McNab code of conduct.

Linny took a deep breath, flicked her scarf over her shoulder, and pushed open the heavy door into the foyer.

Much warmer in here. There was the rich shine of brass fittings everywhere she looked, and the dark gloss of wooden panelling. A reproduction of a famous Scottish painting faced her. Or at least, she assumed it was a reproduction.

Linny gave the doorman a smile as she sailed past towards the reception desk. She probably should have asked Lorne for their room number last night, so that she could avoid all this nonsense, but she hadn't been thinking straight. She was thinking even less straight this morning. She'd been awake most of the night, as usual, and the few occasions when she had dropped off, she found herself dreaming of Nicholas Darlington coming toward her out of the mist. Only as he drew close it wasn't Darlington any more. It was something else. Something monstrous.

Was the dream a warning of things to come? Or had she finally learned caution when it came to the men she was attracted to? Was her brain saying, "Stay away from him, he's not good for you?" Probably not. More likely she was suffering from serious sleep deprivation.

Linny was too tired to work it out right now. She wasn't even certain whether she should have come here, but last night she had made a promise to herself. Somehow when she dragged herself out of bed this morning she'd found the energy to zip on her favourite platform heeled boots. And somehow they had brought her to the door of her sister's posh hotel. Whether she'd wanted them to or not.

"Eh, I'm after Maggie McNab," she said.

The receptionist gave her a snooty look. "Is she expecting you?"

Linny sighed. She just hated it when strangers decided they were gate keepers. "I'm her sister, so

I imagine even if she isn't expecting me she'll see me."

The girl still seemed doubtful and wasn't adverse to letting her know it as she reached for the phone to put through a call.

"Oh hello, Mr Escott," she fluttered.

Mr Escott? She should have asked if the Hellfire Club were leaving off their titles.

"Eh, there's a woman here who says she is Ms McNab's sister. Should I…? Of course, of course."

The girl was positively blushing. Linny sighed again. Whether he called himself Mr Escott or the Marquis of Lorne, the effect was the same. If she didn't know how much Lorne had sacrificed for her sister she would begin to wonder if she shouldn't go upstairs, grab Maggie and run far away. Most guys who had this effect on women made full use of it whenever they could.

"You can go up," said the receptionist in a slightly less prissy voice. "Penthouse suite."

Of course, she thought sarcastically. Nothing was too good for the Sorceress's pets. Linny strolled over the lift and pressed the button. She still felt jittery from too much caffeine, but it was the only way she could keep functioning. On some level, at least.

The lift doors slid smoothly back. Someone was already in there.

Nicholas Darlington leaned against the mirrored wall of the lift. He had forsaken his Regency style clothes for faded blue jeans and a sage green sweater. He was gazing at the floor, leaning on his cane, and seemingly lost in thought. As she came inside he looked up and his eyes widened, then narrowed. But he said nothing.

She found herself at a loss for words, which was unusual. Linny was the queen of the snappy comment. She had an answer for everything. The problem was, right now she didn't know the question.

Perhaps her being at a loss for words wasn't entirely true. She did have one thing she wanted to say, it was just that she knew she shouldn't say it.

How did you get that scar?

It was far too intimate a question, especially when she was trying very hard to keep her distance from this man.

The injury appeared to be very old—a puckered line that began at the corner of his eye, snaked down his cheek, and ended a short distance from the corner of his mouth. A duelling scar, perhaps? Duels were very fashionable at around the time Nicholas was alive, weren't they? Had he called someone out and demanded satisfaction? Or maybe another gentleman had insulted his sister or his mother or his wife—the last of which would open another can of worms for her if it was true.

If she were to give it some thought, and she was trying hard not to, then the conclusion she would come to was that it was Darlington's opponent who had demanded satisfaction, and Darlington himself who had caused the dispute.

"I assume you're going up to the top floor?" His voice was low, husky, and he looked as tired as she felt.

"I've come to see Maggie," she said, in case he had the mistaken impression she'd come to see him.

He stepped aside and waited. "Of course." There went that eyebrow again. She swallowed and, reluctantly, stepped into the lift, which suddenly seemed quite small. He pressed the button to close the door. The signet ring on his little finger caught her eye—something else she wanted to ask him about and wouldn't.

Her gaze now dropped to his Doc Martens. He was resting on his cane as if it was a fashion accessory rather than to aid his movement, but she knew better. How had he injured his leg, and why couldn't it be fixed? She wasn't going to ask that either.

The silence soon became oppressive and Linny rattled into conversation to try and fill it.

"Last night went well. My boss was happy anyway."

Nicholas smiled but his brown eyes were watchful. "I'm glad to have been of help," he said.

"He has your pay at the office, if you want to collect it."

He gave a snort of laughter. "First time in my life I've been paid for an honest day's work."

Silence again. Her nerves jangled and she struggled to keep still. How did he manage to retain that air of cool calm? Maybe she could ask him his secret? Maybe not.

The lift gave a jolt and decided to pause for a

moment. Linny's eyes widened. She wasn't a fan of confined spaces, and although this was hardly a broom cupboard, the dimensions were small enough to make her nervous. When she was a child her father had locked her up for a day and a night on more than one occasion, usually because she said something he didn't like. That did things to a young mind.

Nicholas watched her closely. "It does that rather a lot."

She hoped he couldn't read her thoughts. "Must be strange for you," Linny said, trying to fill the silence. She was nervous, anxious. "All of this I mean," and she waved her arm around her, as if to encompass the world outside the lift.

"I'm getting used to it."

Hmm, maybe he wasn't as cool and collected as she'd thought. One of his Doc Marten's was jiggling up and down. Did he hate being confined in this lift as much as she did, or was he annoyed about something else? Maybe he was just impatient. Suddenly it seemed silly not to ask the questions after all.

"How did you, eh …?" She gestured at her own cheek.

"A duel," he said.

Well, she'd been right about that much!

"Did someone demand satisfaction from you? That was it, wasn't it?"

His eyes met hers and she found she couldn't look away. It was only when the lift jerked upward again that she was able to tear her gaze away. She reached out to clutch onto the brass railing that was fastened at waist height around the interior. Her knuckles were white.

"My past is not something I like to discuss, Linny."

That showed her, then.

They began to move at a creaky snail's pace up through the various levels toward the penthouse. The hotel might look swish from the outside, but Linny suspected it was still old behind the more recent renovations. Victorian, perhaps, so not quite as old as Nicholas Darlington.

She knew he was still watching her, even though she'd looked away. She felt it in the prickle of her skin and the tension in her muscles. Eventually, when the silence was once again too much for her, she turned and faced him. "What?" she demanded.

"You look tired."

"So do you."

"I know why I'm tired. I'm a man from 1808 who has vowed to catch an evil warlock and return him to a Sorceress. That would make anyone lose sleep. I'm wondering though, Linny, why you can't sleep?"

She was about to tell him to mind his own business and instead, to her horror, heard herself blurt out the truth. "I can't sleep because every time I close my eyes whatever came back with me while I was possessed takes another step closer."

He looked shocked, but didn't have time to respond. The door slid open onto the lounge room in the penthouse apartment. Sutcliffe, his big body sprawled on the sofa, looked over and then gave her a grin. Loki gave a bark of joy and ran toward her, barely giving her time to prepare before he leapt onto her, paws on her shoulders.

"And I'm glad to see you too," she said, ruffling his coat. He gave one of those strange doggy replies, as if to say 'Here she is' before he dropped down, trotting back to Sutcliffe, tail wagging.

"Maggie's in her private sitting room," Sutcliffe told her.

Oh is she? Will she receive me now? Linny felt like being a smart arse, but restrained herself. Best to begin politely, even if things didn't end that way.

"Okay dokey."

"Are you doing another ghost tour tonight?" the big man queried. He gave her a hopeful look. "Perhaps I could be the ghost this time?"

Linny pretended to consider his offer. "I'm sure you'd make a very good ghost, Aiden, but we're done with it now. My boss thinks we should draw a line under the *ghost* idea before we get sued."

Sutcliffe thought about that. "But if the man pretending to be the ghost was a different man? That might work." Obviously he wasn't going to give it up easily. She could only think that Sutcliffe was having some kind of withdrawal situation. After the Hellfire Club, and later pursuing a demon around Lorne's estate, he must be craving some excitement. Living in a hotel in Glasgow was obviously far too tame for him.

"You'd be a poor replacement for me." Nicholas stepped up behind her as if staking a claim. "Playing a ghost requires some subtlety, Aiden. I'm not sure you know the meaning of the word."

Sutcliffe sat up straighter, but before he could argue the point, another voice interrupted.

"She's come to see me, boys."

Linny turned. Light poured from a large window in the room behind. Maggie might be little more than a shadowy shape, but she knew her sister too well to think it could be anyone else.

Sutcliffe offered a good-tempered apology. Darlington sank down beside his friend on the sofa and stretched out his bad leg, picking up a controller from the coffee table. "I'm going to thrash you at Grand Theft Auto. Again," he said.

Linny rolled her eyes and joined her sister. Her boots sank into the deep pile carpet with a sensation she could only describe as walking on clouds.

Maggie moved aside, waited for her to enter the room, and closed the door.

The space was massive. Huge windows overlooked the city, which looked sombre today under a slate grey sky. In the room, chintz covered chairs were grouped about a table, and a state-of-the-art entertainment system took up an entire wall. It was hardly the sort of setup the Hellfire Club would be familiar with, apart from the chintz. Then again, she wondered if those 'gentlemen' were welcomed into any of the fashionable drawing rooms of their day, especially wherever respectable ladies were present.

"Come here." Maggie reached for her, and suddenly it was important to hug her little sister as tightly as she could. "Why did you stay away so long?" Maggie sounded as if she was close to tears.

There was a lump in Linny's throat as well. In her five inch platform boots she was the same height as Maggie. She looked her in the eye and tried to come up with some excuses. She couldn't tell her the truth, the fact that she felt she wasn't safe to be with, not any more. She'd been contaminated by something on the other side. The last thing she wanted was for Maggie to be infected too, after all the crap her sister had been through already.

"I'm sorry. I…" She should have prepared a proper excuse, something clever and feasible, instead of just blurting out, "I'm sorry."

Maggie stared at her, seeing far more than Linny wanted her to. Linny responded the only way she could, by turning and walking away, changing the subject as she pretended to admire the room. "You could hold a conference in here," she said with a forced laugh.

"I don't spend much time in here, really." Maggie sank down into an overstuffed chair until it almost swallowed her whole. Linny watched her struggle to push herself upright again, perching on the edge this time. The two sisters looked at each other, then burst out laughing.

"That happens all the time," Maggie complained, wiping the tears from her eyes. "And you should see the bed. In fact…" She stood up and went to another door, flinging it open with a dramatic flourish.

Linny gasped. The bed was massive. A four poster

with red satin and gold braid, and the ripple of purple velvet just to top it off. Obscene, but in a nice way. Maggie laughed at her expression and then turned serious again.

"I feel like I'm dreaming," she said, and lowered her voice. "It can't be real, and yet it is. I'm not sure I'm cut out for this, Linny. I want to work. I *need* to work. It was all right while we were in the between-worlds, I understood it was necessary to stay there to be safe. But now... Everyone is on edge. All this waiting. I find myself wishing it was over, that Stewart was caught and locked away again. Then I remember what that will mean for Lorne. And instead of longing for time to pass quickly, I begrudge every hour ... every *minute*."

She looked so miserable. Linny slid an arm about her and gave her another hug. She would have liked to say something profound, but she was better at snark than insight. Playing down what the future held wasn't much use either—Maggie knew the score where she and her Marquis were concerned. So, in the end, Linny just held her.

"Lorne told me about last night," Maggie said once they had settled down on the overstuffed furniture again. Before Linny could reply, a waiter knocked discreetly on the door and brought in a tray. Linny's stomach rumbled at the sight of the cakes presented, and when he was gone, she tucked in while Maggie poured tea into two delicate cups.

"I haven't had breakfast yet," Linny said, licking the cream off her fingers. "This is delicious, sis."

She heard Loki whine outside the door, but

Maggie ignored him and went back to the subject of her sister's new job.

"Ghost tours? Why would you want to do something like that? After what happened in Lincolnshire, I'd have thought you'd want to keep your distance from the supernatural."

Gee, Maggie, you can't keep your distance from something that followed you back…

"I find it cathartic," she said instead. "And it's not as bad as you think. The tourists are friendly. Yeah, you get the occasional weirdo, but the rest are just after a good time."

Maggie held her cup in two hands. Her voice was full of dry humour. "Nicholas enjoyed it, anyway. We've heard the story so many times now. I think he secretly wants to be an actor. Aiden is jealous. He wants a turn."

"Well, he's not getting one," Linny retorted. "That little drama is over, according to my boss. Next thing all three will be making an appearance and I'll get the sack."

"They're bored," Maggie said, echoing Linny's earlier thoughts. Then her expression changed. "Stewart has been seen at the university."

Linny felt a sinking feeling in her gut. "What happened?"

"He's playing games. Until he comes out into the open, shows his hand, we can't go after him. He always finds a way to disappear."

"You've *seen* him?" she asked, not liking the thought of her sister being in danger. And Stewart was very dangerous indeed.

"I was at the university yesterday and I saw him there. Just for a moment. He was using Simon's body, which makes me so angry." She bit her lip, controlling her emotion. "It's all part of his game and I shouldn't get upset. That's exactly what he wants. But I can't help it."

"Be careful," Linny said, leaning forward, her slice of cake for the moment forgotten. "You can't take any risks, Maggie."

"Believe me, I'm not taking risks. They won't let me. That's why I wasn't there last night to see Nicholas's performance. They insisted I stay home with Loki."

She sounded irritated, but Linny was relieved to hear her sister was being looked after, even if it was against her will. "Where's Lorne now?"

"He went for a walk. Like me, he's sick of being cooped up. He wanted to rent a horse and go for a ride, but I told him that might be a wee bit difficult in the middle of the city."

Linny looked around her again at the sumptuous room. "How are you managing to pay for all of this anyway?"

"The Sorceress. Lorne said it was something to do with Blackfriars and the money from the past being transferred to the present. Allowing for infla-tion. There are a staggering number of zeros after the figures on his bank statement. Don't ask me to explain, I don't understand it. I'm not sure anyone does."

Linny snorted. "Whatever keeps you safe. And before you ask, I'm happy in my own house. I don't need to join you here. I feel safe enough."

Maggie turned to look at her, and she realised that something in her voice had given her away.

"Linny, why would you *not* feel completely safe?"

Chapter Seven

———◆———

"ARE YOU GOING TO FOLLOW me all the way home?"

Of course she should have known she wouldn't get away from the hotel without Nicholas in tow. He was waiting for her in the lobby, and without a word fell into step beside her as she exited the hotel into the crisp Glasgow air.

"I thought I might." He leaned on his ebony cane as he examined her with tea coloured eyes.

"Why?" She spread her arms as if the answer must be out there. Somewhere.

"To help you sleep," he said it almost gently.

Shocked, she blinked. He didn't miss much. He had noticed how sleep deprived she was, and how she really, really didn't want to talk to him about any of that.

I can't sleep because every time I close my eyes whatever came back with me takes another step closer.

He was standing right in front of her now, too close, reading her expression. She really shouldn't have said what she said to him in the lift. Why had she told him? No one knew what she was going through. She hadn't said a word until that moment with him, and she still didn't know why she had done so.

Perhaps it was because he had already seen her at her worst, held her when she was at her most vulnerable. Watched her die and come back to life. Linny trusted him despite her better judgement.

Still that didn't give him the right to think he could dig into her secrets, not in her book anyway.

"I thought you had trouble in the sleeping department yourself," she said, and began to walk along the footpath, but slow enough so that he could keep pace by her side. She didn't want to admit it, not even to herself, but there was some comfort in him being here.

"I don't sleep much, true. Two hundred years in Lorne's family mausoleum, slumbering with his ancestors, tends to put one off closing one's eyes."

She gave a shudder, mostly because he seemed to expect it.

"What you said earlier in the lift … about what came back with you…?" he tried again.

She waved dismissively. "It was nothing. I shouldn't have said anything. Don't worry about it."

"Linny, you don't have to do this alone," he said, and something in his voice—more of that unexpected gentleness—brought tears to her eyes.

She turned away so he wouldn't see and shook her head. "Maggie's insisting I come around for lunch tomorrow. It's my day off."

"So, even the ghosts of Glasgow have days off?" he asked with a straight face.

"They do."

They shared a smile, which was even more disturbing than his empathy. Her blood began to heat up, as if just being this close to him was enough to jump start her hormones.

"Then perhaps I may see you tomorrow. If I am not out hunting our mutual friend Stewart."

There didn't seem to be much to say to that, and staying longer was a very bad idea. Linny began to walk away, quickly this time, so that even if he had wanted to he couldn't follow. She didn't look back.

The further the distance grew between them, the more relieved she felt—or so she told herself. The truth was she didn't feel relieved. She was doing the right thing by keeping her distance, but what she really wanted to do was turn around and beg him to come with her. And if she wasn't a tough and independent woman who needed to protect her little sister, then Linny might have done just that.

Nicholas knew something was wrong. Linny had admitted it to him earlier. But she wasn't the sort to let him into her innermost secrets easily, and he wouldn't have expected her to. And yet, just for a moment, as they stood face to face on the busy Glasgow street, he'd been positive that she wanted to unburden her soul to him.

But when it came to Linny McNab nothing would be easy. She was a woman who trusted few, and relied only on herself. Winning such a woman would be all the sweeter for that.

From the moment she'd stepped inside Maggie's cottage on the night they first met, he knew she was someone he wanted to know. When the Destroyer had almost killed her, he'd felt the agony of her loss, despite their short acquaintance. There had been a connection between them he could not explain, and believing she was gone forever had struck him hard.

Then, when she was saved he had thought, he'd *hoped*, that it was his chance to get to know her in a more conventional manner. Instead, she'd walked away from them all and kept her distance, even now.

Now he realised Linny wasn't just trying to remove herself from what had happened in Lincolnshire. There was more to it than that. When he considered how close the two sisters were, he knew Linny's reason must be an unselfish one. Ergo, she wasn't protecting herself by staying away from her sister, she was protecting her sister by staying away.

Something was very, very wrong.

Nicholas Darlington knew all about wrong, just as he knew about pain. He had suffered it and caused it. His past was like one of Dante's circles of hell. Whatever was troubling Linny would not shock him. He was beyond such things. And perhaps, just perhaps, he might be able to help.

Then again he admitted his need to help wasn't

entirely without self-interest. His attraction to her was growing stronger. He found himself craving more of her. What if he were to take her in his arms and press his mouth to hers? Would she kiss him back, or fight like a she-devil? It had been a long time since he had kissed a woman he wanted the way he wanted Linny. His past was littered with light skirts, women who offered to scratch his itch because they had an itch of their own. Nicholas wasn't about to pretend that he wasn't interested in Linny physically. He wanted her in his arms and in his bed, but he wanted more than that. He wanted a meeting of their minds, and the sweet knowledge that another person in this world might care about what became of him. Just as he did for her.

God help him, he wanted a relationship.

Perhaps it was seeing the deep love Lorne and Maggie had for each other that made him realize he needed the same for himself. He wanted Linny McNab, with her blonde hair and dark flashing eyes, her slim vibrant body, and her sharp tongue. But she also made him laugh, and that was rare indeed for a man like Nicholas Darlington. He wanted someone who would stand beside him on good days and bad, someone who truly understood him, and who he understood just as well. He wondered if that person was her.

He asked himself again, Would Linny allow him to kiss her? His mouth twisted into a smile as he imagined the scene. Perhaps she'd slap his face, or perhaps a blow to the jaw was more her style. In either case he would apologize as best he could and leave her be.

But what if she clung tighter and kissed him back? He'd never had any problems persuading a woman who interested him to take off her clothes, and the thought of this woman lying naked beneath him had occupied his thoughts far more than was comfortable.

He leaned on his ebony cane, feeling the swelling in his trousers. It *had* been a long time. For a moment he allowed himself to picture her fair hair flowing over the bed like a waterfall, her naked body gleaming with sweat as he ploughed into her, driving them both onward to that magical place...

Enough!

Darlington turned back to the hotel, ignoring the uneasy stare from the doorman as he pushed through the door. Linny would be working tonight, and although she'd said she didn't want him there, he reminded himself that she didn't want him there as a *ghost*.

She never said he couldn't trail along as one of the crowd, had she? If he paid for his ticket, who was to stop him keeping an eye on her?

Chapter Eight

MIST LAY MILKY ON THE roads and twirled around the base of the old grey buildings. Perfect ghost hunting weather, thought Linny. Maybe that was why there were twice as many in her group as the previous night, despite Davey having removed mention of their 'ghost' from the advertisement. In fact, there were so many that her boss had had to arrange for a second guide to take the remainder on an alternate route. Word had certainly gotten about that chills were to be had with Glaswegian Ghost Tours.

"All right." She rubbed her gloved hands together for effect but also for warmth. The air was icy, and if it got much colder it might begin to snow. Everyone would be happy just to head to the pub, something that would suit her just fine. A stiff whiskey and a warm fire, and then home and off to bed.

Except for the fact that she couldn't sleep.

"This way now," she called out, raising an arm to attract the attention of the stragglers, and set off with her customers trailing behind her like a conga line of puffer jackets.

She kept to the same route as before. She knew the stories by heart, the words coming out without her even having to think about them. Although she liked to add a little something extra if the faces turned to her began to look bored and their eyes began to glaze over.

Slowly they wound their way through the old part of town, treading carefully on the cobbles. A dog barked from behind a locked gate, which caused a few shrieks followed by relieved laughter. They moved on toward the lane where Nicholas had appeared two nights ago, and she felt a sense of anticipation. What if he was there now despite her warning? What if…?

A man stepped out, barely visible in the mist, despite the glow of the street lamp.

Her heart lifted. He was here after all! Then her heart fell again, as she remembered she had warned him against repeating his performance. She had to put an end to his silly games before she lost her job.

Linny moved to unmask him and realised too late her mistake.

"Hello Linny," said Simon. He said the words in that slightly diffident manner of his, which had been so sweet while he was alive.

She froze, unable to move. Her head knew it wasn't her brother-in-law, because how could it be? Simon was dead, his ashes scattered into the waves at Moyle. This was Stewart. And last time she had encountered him, she had died.

"My, but you are a lovely creature." His voice dropped a little. "You and your sister make quite a pair. Perhaps you would consider changing your allegiance. I can offer you far more than those moth-eaten rakes, you know. In bed and out of it. I have tricks they can only dream of. What do you say?"

She had never considered herself a coward, but neither was she a fool. Linny screamed and turned to run.

As she hoped, the crowd caught her infection and fled for the third night in a row. Only this time they had good reason to, even if they didn't know it. It was only when a pair of arms wrapped around her that she was forced to stop. Fearing Stewart had grabbed her, she struggled frantically, using her elbows to jab into her captor.

"Let go—of me—!" She couldn't seem to get her breath.

"Linny, stop! It's me."

Nicholas?

In a heartbeat she went from not wanting him anywhere near her to being incredibly grateful that he was. But the lack of sleep, worry, and Stewart wearing Simon's body had taken their toll. Linny went into a meltdown.

———◆———

Nicholas got her home. At first she had clung to him, choking on frantic sobs, so he sent those of her group who were left over to the pub, telling them Davey would pay for the first round. That got rid of the stragglers.

"Do you want a drink yourself?" he asked her, concerned by her white face and shaking hands.

"I just want to go home," she whispered. Her dark eyes darted back behind them, into the misty shadows. "Is he gone?"

"Yes. Almost as quickly as he appeared."

He could see that her relief was still tempered by fear. "You saw him too? I wondered if it was only me."

"I saw him," he said.

He hailed them a cab and Linny gave the driver her address. They sat in silence on the ride through the quiet streets. No one with any sense was out and about right now. The night was so cold that he saw frosting on the windows. At first the driver seemed keen to chat, but one glance in the rear-view mirror at Nicholas's face stopped that from continuing.

Good. Nicholas reached across and took Linny's hand. She didn't resist, and her gloved fingers lay in his. He felt tremors running through her. She had reached the edge of a chasm, where one must either jump and accept the consequences, or ask for help. He thought, he *hoped*, she would do the latter.

Once they arrived at the house he followed Linny to the front door, and then followed her inside as she switched on lights. All the lights. Darkness, at the moment, was not her friend. In the kitchen she plugged in the electric kettle. The sound of the boiling water seemed to soothe her, and she stood waiting for the machine to click itself off while she stared at her reflection in the dark window. She snapped the curtains closed.

From the exhausted look of her, Darlington knew she wouldn't be able to stay awake much longer. She needed sleep. Sleep that she was afraid of as much as she yearned for it.

She made the tea and they sat down at the wooden table. There was a bowl of fruit in front of him—apples, oranges and lemons. One of the lemons was beginning to mould, and although he tried to ignore it, in the end he had to remove it and place it in the bin.

She watched him with a half-smile. "I like a domesticated man," she said. Then, her face becoming stark and her eyes wild. "Nicholas, why was Stewart there? I thought it was Lorne he wanted. Why come after me?"

"Because you are Maggie's sister, and Lorne loves Maggie. He wants to unsettle us and what better way to do that than to threaten those we love?"

She nodded as if it made sense, but the fear was still riding her. Despite what he'd said, Nicholas wondered whether there was another reason for Stewart's sudden appearance tonight. Did the American sense his interest in Maggie's sister? Was he playing a deeper game, trying to pick them off one by one? But Stewart's mind was too twisted for him to begin to understand it. He decided it would be best to wait until he could discuss the matter with the others before he assumed the man's motives.

Linny was slumped down in her chair and suddenly she gave a jaw breaking yawn. "I am going to bed," she announced, as if daring whatever was out there to object. And then, her voice turning fragile, she said, "Will you come too?"

He couldn't help but grin at the invitation.

Linny rolled her eyes. "You *know* what I mean," she muttered, her voice weary. "Look, your lordship, if you don't want to stay, that's fine. I understand why you might not want to."

"Linny—"

She held up a hand. "I'm not used to asking for favours, okay? I look after myself and I don't need anyone else to help me. I wouldn't be asking now, but…" She drew a deep breath. "But I think you understand a bit of what I'm going through."

All humour left him. "Not entirely, not yet, but I will stay. Tonight you will sleep, Linny. I promise you that."

She seemed to consider his words, as if questioning his sincerity, and then she said, shakily but with obvious gratitude, "Thank you, Nicholas."

Wearily, she got to her feet and began to leave. He followed but before they reached her bedroom she spun around. "Wait here," she told him. "I'll call you in a minute."

He stopped, and after a moment leaned on his cane. His leg ached but he was used to that. He'd broken it while he was in Italy, and it had never properly mended. The charlatans that passed for healers there hadn't set it until days afterwards, and then it was badly done.

He'd found out later that the doctor who treated him was a friend of the family of the girl who had died. Although the man didn't have the courage to kill him outright, he had been so negligent in his care that for a time Nicholas had been very ill with fever and his life had hung by a thread. When he was well enough to travel, and reached England's shores again, any hope that his own doctor might work some miracle on him was quickly dispelled.

His crooked, painful leg was something to be borne, and so he had borne it all these years. It was the least he could do when he had been responsible for so much worse.

During the Sorceress's long sleep, he'd had plenty of time to ponder his situation. He had committed a terrible wrong and he had been punished for it. Although not, according to the Sorceress, punished nearly enough.

"You must see the error of your ways, Nicholas Darlington." The Sorceress's voice had run like a dark river through his dreams. *"Losing your title, being stripped of your inheritance, was not enough. You have your life, and for me to return it to you I must see a change in you. I know you are capable of so much more than you have shown the world thus far."*

He hadn't known what she wanted from him then. Or perhaps he had, and just wanted to pretend he was blind. It was too difficult, and too painful, to look back over the mess that was his life. To admit that by refusing to face up to his sins, so much potential had been wasted.

"What is the use of going over and over what could have been done differently?" he'd roared at her at one point. *"It is over!"*

"No." Her voice was gentle, although still terrifying. *"You have a chance to make a new life. A chance to start again. How would that feel, Nicholas?"*

He'd said it was a lie and he was done with her, but she would not give up on him. Again and again she appeared in his dreams over those long years of sleep, and slowly his stubborn, turbulent soul had begun to grow calm and pay attention to her.

Darlington had been born bad. At least, that was what his mother said of him. He wished he could go to her now and show her that wasn't true, that he was a new man. A man that she may even have been proud of. Of course, by now she was dust and it was too late to change her mind, and he regretted that fact. He regretted so much, but although his past could never be changed, maybe it was not too late for him to find a future.

"Come in!" Linny's voice startled him back to the present.

He took a deep breath and reminded himself that he was here to help this woman. He had said he would and he genuinely wanted to. He had liked and admired her, right from the moment he met her. But that didn't stop the fact that he also desired her with a hot pulsing need that filled his thoughts with vivid imaginings. He needed to ignore that.

The Sorceress had shown him that he was strong enough not to give in to his baser urges. Had he always been a strong man but been too busy blunting his senses to realise it? Now his head was clear and he did see, and he had hope, although sometimes at night he had doubts as to whether his newfound belief in himself would be enough.

As he opened the door he heard Linny yawn. The bedroom was lit by a small lamp next to the bed and the rest of the room was in shadow. She was tucked up under a white quilt patterned with yellow daisies. This feminine touch was unexpected, but he had begun to realise that Linny was an unexpected sort of woman. Her boots were thrown on the floor and her coat hung over the back of a chair with other sundry items of clothing. A large toy bear sat in a corner, one of the football scarves he'd come to recognise as Glasgow Celtic tied about its neck. He wondered if it was left over from the days when Keith and Linny were a couple—Keith had been wearing the same coloured jersey. He noticed that the bear was smiling, but he didn't trust it.

"Take off your shoes," Linny murmured. He heard her yawn again. The top of her head was visible above the quilt, and the shape of her beneath it. Darlington hesitated and then sat down, laying aside his cane, and took off his Doc Martens. He left the rest of his clothing in place. It was chilly in the bedroom and he wasn't sure if she expected him to cuddle up under the quilt with her. Probably not. They were acquaintances through adversity, and in her mind he was only here because she was too desperate to refuse his offer of help. That he found her almost irresistibly attractive wasn't part of the equation, if she was even aware of the fact.

He needed to tread carefully. Linny had been hurt, and she kept her heart tucked deep inside stone walls she believed would protect her. Nicholas needed to show her he could be trusted, that he had her welfare in mind and he would put her first. He had to break down those walls, climb inside, and persuade her to let him stay. Unlike the shallow, careless man he used to be, he needed to use his brain instead of his cock.

Nicholas eased himself full length onto the bed and leaned back against the pillows, so that he was almost sitting up with his legs outstretched. The mattress was soft and he sank down into it. Not what he was accustomed to, but it was tolerable. He'd slept in far worse places. Nicholas closed his eyes, but the light was still there, shining through his eyelids.

He reached across her, and switched off the lamp.

Linny jerked upright as if she'd been shot. "No, no! Leave it on!"

Fumbling with the switch, he did as he was told. With the light back on he could see clearly just how frightened she was. Her dark eyes were full of terror and her skin was leached of colour. He tried not to notice the soft baby blue nightshirt that was all that covered her nakedness. A caring friend, he reminded himself sternly, would ignore such temptation.

"I thought—" he began to explain.

"I need to see," she interrupted. She took a deep breath as she tried to calm herself. "When I know it's there—that's bad enough—but if I can't *see* it…" Her shudder was very real.

"Hush," he soothed. "I'm here to watch out for you. Close your eyes, and sleep. Go on," he insisted when she stared at him as if she might refuse. "You're safe."

He could see she was considering some kind of retort, but it seemed she was too tired and just didn't have the energy to go through with it. She slid down under the quilt but kept her face above it and turned to him. Her eyes remained open.

Was that because she didn't quite trust him, or because it gave her comfort to see him here, watching over her? He hoped it was the latter but feared it might be the former.

He folded his arms. His bad leg was comfortable, so he moved it until it wasn't. The subtle ache, he knew from experience, would keep him from falling asleep.

"Why aren't you a lord anymore?" she asked in a sleepy, curious voice.

"I was stripped of my title."

"They can do that?"

"My family could, yes."

She made a noise through her nose. "I don't like the sound of that. What was your title before they took it off you? Your full title?"

He wondered why she wanted to know, or why he should tell her, but neither seemed important enough for him to refuse. "Nicholas Darlington, Earl of Northcote and Viscount Haymere." The words sounded strange to him now, as if he was speaking of someone else. In a way, he was.

She blinked. For a moment he thought she was actually impressed by his titles. He should have known better.

"So, you really were a posh toff," she murmured, and yawned again. "A Marquis *and* an Earl. What was it with you guys that you had to muck up your lives by playing at a Hellfire Club?"

"You are mistaking the man I was then with the man I am now," he answered.

"Am I?" Her gaze dropped to his mouth. "I wouldn't know. I'm just trying to understand who exactly I'm sharing my bed with."

He wished she wouldn't look at him like that, so very sexy and rumpled. He forced his thoughts above the quilt. "You are sharing your bed with a man who wants to help you, Linny. A man you can trust."

"Trust, eh?" she muttered, but there was a curve to her lips that made him believe she thought well of his answer.

"Call me Darlington," he suggested. "Or Nicholas, if you prefer. That is my name now, plain and simple."

"Nicholas," she repeated softly. She yawned. "I still want to know what you did that was so terrible. Don't think you can put me off that easily, *Nicholas*." Her eyelids dropped further and she snuggled deeper into her nest. "I've never met an Earl before, not even an *ex* Earl."

"I am just a man."

"A two hundred year old man," she countered.

"Who no doubt went to the best schools his family could afford."

"Well, there is that," he admitted.

"I didn't even finish high school," she said. "I was too busy looking after Maggie. She was so bright and clever, I wanted her to succeed."

"You did a good job."

Her tired face brightened a little. "I did, didn't I? All those hours at the supermarket and working at a bar until one in the morning, it was all worth it. I put my dreams on hold, sure, but I don't regret it."

"And what are your dreams?" He'd asked her that before and he wondered if this time she'd answer.

"I want to help people. People like me and Maggie. Social work, maybe. Go home at night with some sense of satisfaction, even if the pay isn't great. I'd have to go back to school. Study." She yawned. "Not sure I'm clever enough, though. That's Maggie's strength."

"If you are passionate about something, you can do it," he said quietly. "And who says you're not clever enough? You could do anything you set your mind to."

She smiled, her eyes now half closed. "Thank you, Nicholas. One day I hope you'll trust me enough to tell me what you did to lose your title."

Her eyes closed at last, and he was glad when he heard her soft even breathing, indicating she had finally given in to sleep. He hadn't wanted to tell her what he'd done, and hoped she would forget the question, although knowing Linny that seemed unlikely. Perhaps he should lie? Find a more acceptable story to pacify her curiosity? But that wasn't the man he was now. These days nothing but the truth would do for Nicholas Darlington.

The room was cool but not uncomfortably so, and once or twice he found he'd begun to doze off. He forced himself awake. Counting virgins helped, counting virgins leaping over a fence was even better. Although the more he counted, the more they seemed to look like Linny, and he was fairly certain she would not qualify. It was quite amusing however and kept him awake.

Darlington was drifting into sleep and it was a moment before he came to with a start, noticing how cold the room had become. By then his breath was white, and his fingertips had become nubs of ice. Linny hadn't moved, but there was a crease in her smooth brow. Was she having a bad dream? He moved to touch her and she made a little sound, twisting her head away, her hands clasping the edge of the quilt.

That was when he became aware of another presence. Felt it rather than saw it. His senses were already trying to warn him as he swept his gaze around the room, trying to pierce the shadows.

Something was in the corner, close to the untrustworthy bear. A smudge of darkness that looked darker than its surroundings. It was wrong, and he knew at once it shouldn't be there.

Instead of approaching it, Darlington kept very still and waited to see what would happen next. The darkness began to take form.

First a shoulder, furred and muscular, then a

head, bent low as if it was shy. Or sly. Ears that were pointed, and legs folded up against its chest. It was crouching, unmoving, but Darlington never doubted for a moment that it was aware. He suspected that any moment it might spring toward him. He was ready for that, ready to throw himself in front of it and protect the woman at his side.

Linny stirred again and moaned in her sleep, but he didn't take his eyes from the corner.

The thing lifted its head.

Despite the gloom he could see that this was nothing like the Destroyer, with its yellow hair and pointy teeth. This was something new, and it wasn't interested in him. It looked past him, focussed entirely on Linny, and as it turned its head in her direction, its eyes seemed to glow with pale and malevolent luminosity.

He must have made an involuntary movement, because suddenly it was looking directly at him. He could read the fury in those bulging eyes. He was interfering in something he had no business in, or at least that was the impression it was trying to convey.

And then it was gone.

He turned his head, thinking perhaps it had moved to a different part of the room, but he couldn't see it anywhere. The sensation he had felt when it appeared had gone too. All the same, Darlington climbed off the bed and approached the corner to take a closer look.

Nothing. Just that unpleasant looking bear in an ugly scarf.

After checking the rest of the bedroom, he walked over to the door and opened it. The house was silent and he was fairly certain it was empty. However, just to be sure, he walked through and began to check into all the nooks and crannies.

His sense that the thing was gone had been correct.

But would it come back? He was certain it would, and he needed to discover why it had chosen Linny. He needed to understand what plans it had for her.

"Nicholas!"

Linny's voice carried from the bedroom, the sound high and anxious.

Had the creature returned? Nicholas ran, catching hold of the doorjamb as he came through the doorway. His leg wasn't used to running but he ignored the jolt of pain and concentrated on the woman in the bed.

Linny was sitting up, her arms wrapped around herself, shivering violently. Dark eyes, enormous and terrified, were fixed on the corner of the room where the creature had been crouched only moments before. Even as he came toward her, he was processing this. She *knew*. Just as the creature had some connection with her, then she had a bond with it.

"I'm here." He sank down on the bed and reached for her. "It's all right, I'm here." She came into his arms without protest and buried her face into his chest. He rested his face against her hair and breathed in, aware of her both her strength and her fragility.

"I dreamed... I thought..." Her voice was breaking. "I thought there was something there, in the corner. *Crouched.*"

She lifted her head and looked at him as if for confirmation. "Nicholas? Did you see it too?"

He thought about a comforting lie, but that would not help her. Part of her fear was based on certainty. Wondering whether what she was seeing in her dreams was real, or if she was going mad. So he did the only thing he could do now. He told the truth.

Chapter Nine

——

"I SAW SOMETHING."

Linny leaned away so that she could see Nicholas's face while he spoke. If he had been like most of the men she'd known growing up, he'd have handled her with kid gloves, glossed over the truth with a comfortable lie. But Linny wasn't a kid gloves type of girl, even when things were looking really bad. Instead, when she stared into his light brown eyes, she saw a streak of honesty there that was as refreshing as it was unsettling.

This man would never lie to her. Not like her ex-husband or her father.

That was a good thing. Of course it was. She craved honesty like she craved Tunnock's caramel wafers. But this wasn't an ordinary situation. This wasn't a "did you take fifty quid from my purse?" kind of situation. Being honest now would only confirm her worst nightmares.

"*Something*?" she repeated, fixing him with a hard gaze. "What was this *something*?"

His gaze dropped down and then up again.

Linny followed it, wondering if what he'd seen had been on her, and only then realised her nipples had turned into hard little buds in the cold air, perfectly visible through her cotton top. She folded her arms but he had already moved on.

"It formed over there." He pointed toward the corner where Keith's bear resided. The one he'd bought for her in the early days of their relationship. She wasn't sure why she'd kept it—she didn't even like Celtic. "First it was a shadow, then a shape and then a being. It was only there for a moment before it noticed me and vanished."

Goosebumps prickled her skin and she nodded.

"I wondered if it might have moved elsewhere in your house. That was what I was looking for when you woke up. But whatever it was, it seems to have gone back to wherever it came from."

For now.

She heard the words in her head, though he hadn't spoken them aloud. She dug deep, took hold of what remained of her courage, and forced out another question she really didn't want to ask. "What did it look like?"

"An animal of sorts, and yet I think it had intelligence. Or cunning. Physically, it had pointed ears and a short, strong body. It was sitting on its haunches, over in the corner, head down, and when it looked up—the eyes—"

"They glowed," she whispered.

He nodded. "Yes, they did."

"Oh God. Oh God, it's real!" Linny's voice rose to a screech that made Nicholas wince. "That *thing* is real. I kept hoping it was a dream, some fragment of memory from the other side, but I knew. Who am I kidding? I knew all along it was real."

"This is why you kept yourself apart from Maggie? This has been happening since the Destroyer?"

She nodded. "Right from the first night I returned, I felt … contaminated."

He stared into her eyes and she wasn't sure whether it was sympathy or empathy she saw there.

"This thing…" he began.

She swallowed, and tried to gather her scattered thoughts.

"We need to find out what it is and then we need to find out what it wants."

Nicholas spoke as if this was an everyday occurrence. Then again, this was someone who had had his share of demons and Sorceresses, and had slept in a tomb for two hundred years.

"And how are we going to do that?" she croaked. "Ask it next time it comes to visit? Send it an invitation? 'Join the Hellfire Club for drinks and nibbles?'" She was on the verge of hysteria, full of manic energy.

He smirked. "The Hellfire Club was more of a chalice of red followed by an orgy type of organisation."

"God, tell me you didn't say that," she groaned. It was wrong, she knew it was wrong, but there was a bonfire of desire burning inside her. An orgy with him? Yes, please. She knew what he had been like in the bad old days, but this man, the man beside her right now—she wanted *him*.

He took a deep breath. He must have sensed how she was feeling. Well, of course he did. How many women had he seduced over the years, and how many had seduced him? Linny was no stranger to one night stands or temporary relationships. She'd tried to change all that with Keith, she really had, but one thing marriage had taught her was that it wasn't for her. After the divorce, her life had been reduced to casual hook ups.

But this didn't feel like a hook up. This felt like a long slow burn and once the fuse was lit there would be no putting it out. It would burn on until whatever it was between them had been extinguished.

His hand rested upon her face, his thumb brushing against her lips as if he wanted to open them up so he could dive right in. She could see it in the way his eyes blazed, and the flush along his cheekbones. His breath was warm upon her skin and she realised he was closer now, leaning in.

His lips were fuller than she'd thought, and softer. They brushed over hers and she heard herself sigh with longing. Need. Her nipples wanted his mouth on them and the hot ache between her legs longed to be assuaged. She hadn't been this hot for a man since … well, she'd never been this hot for a man.

"Linny," he said, low and raspy. "I want you. I want you in my bed, but know that I want you out of it, too. I want all of you."

She blinked. He was saying something she should be listening to. "You want all of me?"

"But you have to want all of *me*. I'm done with

drunken shags and women whose names I've forgotten by morning."

She barely registered his words at first. "Do you mean the whole…?" *Romance thing,* she meant to say, but cut herself short. Could Nicholas Darlington, the Regency rake, really want that? Her heart gave a hard thump and suddenly she found herself breathless, and she wasn't sure whether it was because she was yearning for something she couldn't have, or she was afraid that if she did get it she would stuff it all up.

She leaned back. He really was serious. And then the rest of his words finally sank in. Did he think she just wanted him for a quickie? Well, to be fair, she had been considering that, hadn't she? Her success rate when it came to long term relationships was pretty much nil. He couldn't have known that she had been infatuated with him since they first met and had simply refused to act on it, could he? Even then, she'd sensed that to involve herself with this man would be dangerous to her heart. What Nicholas was saying was sensible. And he was right to stop them from what could end up a disastrous mistake without considering the potential fallout.

Linny's hair fell into her face as she shook her head. She needed to shut this down.

"This isn't the time for this conversation," she said in her best no-nonsense voice. "Assuming there ever is a time."

He moved back and gave them both some space. "Very well. If that's how you feel." His face was hard, his expression a blank wall. A moment ago he'd seemed all in with where their kiss might lead, but now?

She refused to blame herself. If he was going to turn cold fish, that was on him. She was doing him a favour, after all. He was better off without her.

She cleared her throat. "What will we do? About that … that…" She pointed at the wall where the creature had appeared in her dream, and apparently in reality as well.

"We will talk to the others. We may need to consult the Sorceress. Providing she'll even allow herself to be summoned."

"Is that really necessary?" Linny remembered her previous encounter with that nightmare of a woman. The two of them hadn't got on, and that wouldn't exactly be advantageous now that she needed advice. Would she ever learn to keep her mouth shut?

"It might be. This creature is beyond my ken." Darlington was still speaking in a thoughtful, pedantic way, as if he hadn't just been on the verge of joining her in an orgy for two. She could imagine him in Parliament, addressing the nation. And furthermore, she could imagine the nation listening. "We have to find out if this creature poses a threat and if so, to whom."

Linny forced her tired and confused mind to consider his words. Did that horrible creature pose a threat? Given where she'd picked up her hitchhiker, she didn't see any logical alternative. Otherwise why was the very thought of it putting a stop to her sleep? Some ancient alarm system inside her head was warning her not to slip too deep into unconsciousness. Because if she did then the animal would creep closer and closer and then… She shivered violently.

Nicholas gave her a look of concern while his hand hovered briefly over her shoulder. Then he drew back. No more touching. It seemed a pity, but she had to draw a line between them.

"Did it say anything?" Linny asked, trying to stay on point. "I suppose it didn't happen to explain to you what it was doing in my bedroom?"

He shook his head. "As soon as it noticed me it was gone."

"So either it's frightened of you or it doesn't want you here when it does whatever it wants to do to me."

He seemed as though he was about to say something, then changed his mind. "I think what this shows is that you need us around you. You can't be on your own, Linny. Not anymore."

He was right. Much as she would have liked to play stubborn, insist that she could take care of herself just as she always had, she needed help. But relying on other people was unfamiliar territory for Linny, and she wasn't happy about it.

"But if I stay with you guys, I'll only be bringing the danger to you?"

Nicholas's sombre face lightened into a familiar smile, and she was able to breathe again. "Linny, consider what you're saying. Do you think none of us have faced danger? We are under threat all the time. We need to stay together. All of us. There is safety in that."

He was right but arguing was in her nature. "I don't—"

He put his index finger against her lips. "Just this once, please, do as I say," he growled.

Her eyes widened. So many smart comments she could make, all of them to disguise the fact that her breathing had quickened and her pulse was beating double time. Instead she scowled and pushed his finger away. "I'll get dressed and pack some things," she muttered.

He squeezed his hand into a fist and stared at her, and only seemed to catch onto her meaning when she waved a hand for him to leave. "My apologies," he said, and eased himself off the bed, limping to the door and closing it behind him.

She felt wrung out, but there was just so much time she could spend inside her own head. Nicholas Darlington had offered her all of himself and she had turned him down like a bad credit card.

"Come on, girl. Get your act together."

She climbed out of bed and began to throw some clothing into a suitcase. Jeans and sweaters, mostly. It wasn't likely she'd need any sparkly evening gowns. Not that she had any.

Once she was dressed, and had brushed the tangles out of her hair, she left the bedroom to collect the remainder of her necessities.

Darlington stood by the sitting room window as she passed by him on her way into the bathroom. He'd left the seat up, she noticed. *Two hundred year old man and he still can't remember to put down the toilet seat! Typical.* She tried to whip up some rage, but her heart just wasn't in it.

She gathered together her bottles and tubes, her make-up, as well as her toothbrush and paste. Was there anything else? She looked about the small, claustrophobic room with its out-of-date tiles and ever present mould, and suddenly found herself deeply depressed.

Why is this happening to me? What have I done to deserve this?

A hint of movement in the mirror caused her to jump, thinking the creature was back again. It was Nicholas, standing in the doorway behind her. Despite his modern clothing, he might have been a ghost come from the past, but Linny knew this was very much a man of flesh and blood.

Right now she needed the touch of a man, just as she needed the pleasure and distraction that being with someone like him could give her. Sex was a way of getting all this out of her head. But he had that damned condition. No casual sex for Lord Darlington, no sir.

Still, she wanted him. But *all* of him? Was that even possible? Could she say yes and allow herself to follow her desires? He was a complex man. It was possible he would want a great deal more than she could give. More than she was capable of giving.

If she was honest with herself, the two of them would be a recipe for disaster.

She shook her head, and thanked God she'd come to her senses before she travelled down that road. One Regency rake in the family was quite enough, thank you very much.

And yet she wasn't happy. She hadn't been happy for some time now. When she'd made the trip to Lincolnshire she'd been thinking seriously of returning to her studies, even if she had to work at night to pay her way. She wanted more from life, and she'd decided she was going to go after it. Then, after Lincolnshire, all her thoughts had been occupied with her nightmare companion, and the need to keep her distance from Maggie.

But Nicholas had known she was in trouble, and had refused to take no for an answer. He'd insisted she tell him the truth. He had run her to ground until she gave in. She admitted she was more than a little bit infatuated.

Just for a moment, her lips seemed to burn where his mouth had brushed against hers. They could be in her bed now, hot and sweaty, enjoying each other. But a relationship? She would end up making him miserable and herself too.

Linny took a steadying breath and glanced at him as if she'd only just noticed him. "Nearly ready," she said briskly, and picked up a couple more things. She brushed past him as she left the room, and studiously ignored that zing of attraction she continued to feel. Adding what was in her arms to her suitcase, she closed the lid with a snap.

Her boots were in the sitting room. He silently watched her as she sat down to pull them on.

This was getting nerve wracking. At least when they got to the hotel the others would be there, and that might dilute whatever this chemistry was when she was around Nicholas. She hoped so because if this sexual tension got any hotter she was going to find herself in real trouble.

"I'll call a cab," she said as she stood up. Once that was done, she locked up her house, and they went outside to wait.

Her neighbours were asleep, their houses in darkness, and the night was bitterly cold. Flakes of snow were falling into the street and sticking, creating a thin layer of white. Snow always made everything look so clean and pure, but Linny knew nothing about this world was pure. There was dirt under that snow. There always was.

Linny glanced at her house and wondered if she would see it again. She was about to launch into the unknown, like some Charles Dickens character. Cold and frightened and alone. Though maybe she wasn't quite alone.

Linny edged closer to the man at her side. He might be hot and he might be a puzzle, and she might struggle to keep everything between them PG, but right now she was very glad that he was there.

Chapter Ten

A S HE EXITED THE LIFT into the penthouse, Nicholas knocked his cane against a chair that had been left in the way. The noise wasn't too loud, but it was enough to wake Loki from his slumber on the white leather sofa.

The wolf-like dog sat up, made one of those strange yawning noises that he saved for his new best friends, and launched himself at Linny. She gave a squeal and fell back onto the thick pile carpet. Loki turned into one giant wriggle and his tongue lashed at her face no matter how much she tried to avoid it.

Nicholas tried to help her fend off the dog, but all Linny could do was laugh. The pent up tension he had felt between them was bubbling out of her, which was for the best. He didn't know why he hadn't just shagged her and got it out of his system. A casual dalliance was obviously what she had wanted, and from what he knew of these future times, hardly looked down upon at all. But no, he'd had to lay down the law about what he expected between them.

But Linny had been hurt too many times to take a chance on someone like him so soon. He understood that. But he had been hurt too, and he was trying to become a better man, and as such he had to be fair to himself as well as her. Darlington didn't want a one night stand, or even several nights. He wanted to keep her, and she needed to accept that and come to him with her eyes open wide.

They were tangled on the floor now, and Loki was enjoying their play immensely. Nicholas moved to grab the dog by the scruff at the same time as Linny, and they bumped heads.

She rubbed at her skull. "Ouch!" He cupped his hand over the spot, peering into her face. For a moment their eyes met. He wanted to apologise, to explain why he had said what he said earlier. He was possessed by an insane urge to bare his soul to her, to risk everything on a toss of the dice, even if it meant she might walk away and never look at him again.

The overhead light turned on and they all froze.

Lorne stood outside the door to his private rooms, hand still on the switch. His black jeans were slung low on his hips and his chest was bare. He seemed unimpressed.

"Some of us are trying to sleep."

"My apologies." Nicholas got awkwardly to his feet, holding fast to the still playful Loki. Linny also stood up, clearly wishing herself miles away from all this.

"Did we wake you?" she asked awkwardly. Nicholas fought back a smile. Unlike most of the staff in this building, Linny wasn't the sort to ogle Lorne and toss her hair about for him. It seemed she saved her ogling for him, or at least she had until she'd put a hold on whatever was developing between them.

"You woke Maggie," Lorne informed them. He moved forward, noting the suitcase. "Not Sutcliffe though, it would seem. Only a cannon could wake him." He stopped, looking from Darlington to Linny and back again, and waited for their explanation.

"Linny has come to stay with us," Nicholas said. "Maggie invited her, remember?"

"I remember." Lorne waited a beat. "Where is she going to sleep tonight? With Loki on the sofa?"

"She will sleep in the small bed chamber."

"And you'll take the sofa?"

Nicholas hesitated. "Linny would prefer not to sleep unattended tonight."

Linny butted in, shooting him an anxious look. "How small is this small bed chamber, Nicholas?" she said in an undertone that was clearly agitated. "Would it be just us?"

Lorne appeared suddenly very interested but Nicholas ignored his stare. "Sutcliffe shares his room with Loki," he explained to Linny.

"Might be rather crowded in there," Lorne commented unhelpfully.

Nicholas ignored him. "You and I can take the smaller room, if that is acceptable to you."

Linny was quick to agree, which showed him

just how frightened and desperate she must be. A
woman like Linny McNab would not easily admit
to needing a man, not unless she was at her wit's
end. A man, he reminded himself, who she had put
in the friend region, or area. He'd forgotten the
exact expression. She needed him, yes, but she was
not about to trust him beyond that.

He supposed he couldn't blame her. He pointed
her in the right direction and, her back stiff, she
made her way to the door, reached in to flick on
the light, and then closed it firmly after her.

"I will join you in a moment," Nicholas said after
her. He then turned to his friend. "It's not what
you're imagining."

Lorne's smile broadened. "I can imagine quite a
lot, Nicholas."

"I'm sure you can. But there's something you
need to know about her, something that affects us
all."

"Very well." He folded his arms and waited. Loki,
without Linny around to torment, trotted back to
his sofa.

"When Linny was possessed by the Destroyer, I
believe her soul went somewhere…" He shrugged
awkwardly. "I don't know yet where; she hasn't
said a great deal on the matter. But when she was
returned to her body, we thought all was well."

"And clearly it wasn't."

"She brought something back with her. A creature. I saw it, for a brief moment. It comes when
she sleeps, but so far she's been able to wake herself
before it can do whatever it intends to do to her."

"And what does it intend to do?"

"I don't know that either, but its intentions can hardly be a benevolent. Tonight I was watching over her while she slept, and it saw me."

"What did it look like?" Lorne asked.

He proceeded to describe it, but his friend shook his head, as perplexed as Darlington. "Not the Destroyer then. That's something to be thankful for."

"But what if it's something worse?" countered Nicholas. "I'm worried. What will happen if Linny can't wake herself up and I'm not there?"

Lorne frowned, considering the possibilities. "It wants her for some reason we do not yet understand."

"I can't imagine there are any good reasons," said Nicholas. "More importantly, I don't believe we can take the risk."

"No, we can't take any risks. Not now. We have Stewart to capture and this is a complication. Unless this is another of his tricks?"

The two men stood together in silence.

"What do you intend to do?" Lorne asked him finally.

That Lorne, who had always been the leader of their little group, should ask what *he* intended to do came as a surprise, though perhaps it shouldn't have. The two of them had come a long way in the two hundred years they had been locked away, and when they had captured the Destroyer they had moved even closer toward the men they were striving to be. Now Nicholas had his own ideas, and he wasn't afraid to speak them out loud.

"We need the Sorceress. She might have the answers."

The last time he had seen her was when she had allowed them to leave the between-worlds, to continue their pursuit of Stewart. She had sent them on their way and reminded them yet again that they needed to place the ring upon Stewart's finger to secure him. As far as Darlington was aware, Lorne always carried it somewhere about his person.

"You could try to request her presence," Lorne said. "Although she may decide not to come. She is a law unto herself."

"Rather like the McNab sisters."

The comment made Lorne smile, but only for a moment.

"I will try to speak with her," Nicholas announced. "I think I must. In the meantime, I need to keep watch over Linny whenever she sleeps. She is in our care and we cannot fail her."

Lorne gave him a look. "You can't do it all yourself, Nicholas, you know that. Tomorrow we'll work out a timetable."

He wanted to argue. He felt it was his place alone to protect this woman, but he also knew Lorne was right.

"We'll talk tomorrow," he said at last, and headed for the small bedroom, lugging Linny's suitcase behind him.

What in God's name had she packed in there? Rocks?

Linny was in the bed, eyes closed. She lay on her

back, the blanket up to her underarms, and as far as he could tell she was naked. *Well that is interesting.* Then he remembered that her night garments were probably in the suitcase he carried. *So, not an invitation to wild passion after all.* Though he supposed she could have slept in her clothes.

With a wry smile, he quietly set the case down and out of the way.

The room was small compared to the others in their suite, but still larger than the bed chamber in Linny's house. She had drawn the curtains across the large windows, which screened the view of the city and left only the muted sound of traffic from the street far below. Traffic, he thought, with a shake of his head, was not what it used to be. In his day it consisted of horses and carriages, wagons and barouches. Now there was nothing but motorised vehicles that puffed out noxious fumes, travelling at unsafe speeds, and people who swore and waved their fists at each other if one of them was the slightest bit slow at a green light.

In some ways, like this, the world had changed for the worse. In other ways, well, he knew it was better. *He* was better. And Linny was here in this modern world with him, so surely that was a good thing?

Nicholas turned back to the room and took a good look around, checking every shadow, just in case. But he saw nothing out of the ordinary. Nothing hiding, waiting to leap out at them. Everything appeared to be just as it should.

He had thought Linny was asleep until she spoke.

"Thank you for doing this." She sounded a little bit irritated, as if she would rather not have to thank anyone.

"It is my pleasure," he said, with a slight bow. Such courtesies were still instinctive to him. Perhaps they were in his DNA—another modern term he'd picked up. In his time he would have said "in his blood." He had learned the mannerisms of a gentleman from birth, and it was difficult to unlearn them.

Her dark eyes sparkled up at him. "You're the only man I know who has ever bowed to me," she said. "Next time I'm on my feet I might just curtsey back."

"I know it is not the way of people these days," he said a little defensively. "Women do not expect special treatment. In fact, according to Maggie, they can be insulted if one tries."

"It's a little more complicated than that," Linny replied, and yawned. "But don't worry, I'm not insulted."

He wasn't sure what to say to that, so he looked around and found a comfortable chair.

"What are you doing?" she asked.

"I can hardly sleep in the bed with you."

"Why not?" The irritation was back in her voice. "Because we didn't shag? Nicholas, I won't be able to sleep at all if I keep thinking of you being uncomfortable in that chair. I know your leg pains you. It does, doesn't it?"

"I barely notice it," he lied, but he limped over to the bed anyway.

This mattress wasn't as soft as Linny's, and he tucked some pillows in behind him, and made himself as comfortable as possible sitting up. His leg did ache, of course it did. Sometimes the ache was constant, a low level throb that wouldn't go away no matter what he did. On nights like that Darlington often resorted to the claret. At other times the pain was so bad there was no comfort to be had at all. Those were the worst, because with the pain came the memories as to why he deserved it. Sometimes the memories hurt more than his leg.

She watched him through her long lashes, and he wondered if she had read his thoughts. He hoped not. Right now he wanted neither her questions nor her pity. Especially not her pity. He needed her to trust him, and being an object of her pity would not gain him that. Besides, he still had his pride.

Perhaps she read his withdrawal in his face, because she turned abruptly away from him and wriggled into a more comfortable position. "Good night, Nicholas. Keep the monsters away, would you?"

Darlington smiled. "Of course." He flicked on the small bedside lamp and then turned off the overhead light. He didn't make the mistake of turning them both off. Not this time.

After a short while he knew by Linny's soft breaths that she was asleep.

Nicholas folded his arms and prepared himself to guard her until dawn.

Chapter Eleven

———

L INNY WOKE, STRETCHED OUT LIKE a cat, and opened her eyes. It was morning. At least, that's what the grey light that slipped beneath the curtain was telling her. She was alone in the bed and couldn't believe how much better she felt. Her sleep may have been short, but it had been deep and refreshing. Now it was as if she was a new person.

Nicholas sitting beside her, guarding her, watching over her—whatever you wanted to call it—had made an enormous difference. He was her friend, or at least she hoped so, and for that she was grateful to him. She just wished things hadn't become so complicated. Linny didn't like complicated when it came to men, which was why she preferred to skim the surface. What was wrong with spending some time together, both of them getting the satisfaction they wanted, and still be free to move on? So what if those kind of hook-ups felt empty? Empty was better than messy and painful. Until recently, Linny had been all for it.

Until Nicholas Darlington, Regency rake and living bicentennial man, came along.

Speaking of which, where was he? She sat up, spied her suitcase and was about to get out of bed and put on some clothes, when the door opened.

Nicholas walked in with a mug of coffee. His face was a frown.

"For me?" she asked.

He started at the sight of her awake, then approached the bed. She dragged the quilt higher over her chest. Last night she had been so tired. She'd left her suitcase out in the sitting room, so she had stripped off and climbed into bed. It had seemed a good idea at the time, but right now was starting to feel rather awkward.

"You're awake."

"I am."

His dark eyes examined her bare shoulders before they slid back to her face. He looked rumpled and sleepy, and there was something very appealing about the whole package. If he hadn't given her that relationship ultimatum she would have reached out and pulled him down into the bed with her. In fact, she would probably have done so last night. There was a spark between them, and she knew the sex would be incredible.

Pity it was never going to happen. Not so long as there were strings attached.

"Did it come back last night?" she asked as Nicholas handed over his mug.

"No."

"What do you think that means? Did you scare

it off?"

"I don't know. I doubt it's given up, Linny. You shouldn't think that."

She sighed and sipped with care. "No, I guess not." The coffee was good and hot, and sweet, just as she liked it. A point of similarity between them. She wondered if that meant anything. Her ex had liked his coffee black and bitter, and that should have been a warning to her, but at the time she'd been too full of starry eyed attraction to take heed.

"How do you feel?" Nicholas asked.

"Fabulous!" she assured him after she'd drunk half the mug. "Like my old self."

His mouth cracked into a smile, but his eyes examined her as if she was one of Maggie's archaeological finds. She wished he was easier to read, but she supposed that the mystery was part of the attraction. Nicholas was all deep waters.

She noticed the dark circles under his eyes and the gaunt look to his face. "You look just about done in." Even his scar was more prominent when he was tired. She wondered if it had happened at the same time as his leg injury? Or was Darlington just clumsy? She thought about saying the joke out loud, but right now she doubted he would appreciate it. In any event, it was Darlington who made a joke.

"I had no sleep, remember? And I'm older than you. A *lot* older."

She chuckled appreciatively as she sipped at the coffee. "Yeah, you bicentenarians need your naps, I'm sure. You'd better take the bed then," she said.

"I'll go and see what's happening with Maggie."

He didn't need to be asked twice. He climbed onto the bed and closed his eyes with a sigh.

"Ahem. I need to get dressed first," she reminded him.

He didn't move. He looked as if he'd fallen into instant sleep. She prodded him with a finger to make sure, but apart from a fleeting frown he remained unconscious.

Okay. She slid out from under the covers and glanced back, but his eyes were firmly shut and his mouth slightly open. He was definitely asleep. She went to the suitcase and found what she needed. Black tights and a short black skirt, a turquoise sweater. Perfect. Linny put them on and gave her hair a quick brush. Her teeth and face would have to wait until she checked out the bathroom. She hoped she didn't have to take turns with Sutcliffe and Loki… Maybe she could use Maggie's en-suite?

She had her hand on the doorknob when she felt the irresistible urge to look back at her new—and also very old—friend. Some men looked helpless when they were asleep, like lost little boys. Nicholas Darlington didn't. Even asleep he had a smouldering look. Her sleep must have revitalized her hormones because those tingles she had felt last night were back and multiplying.

How are we going to spend our nights here, alone together?

Against her better judgment she reached out and brushed her fingertips over his scruffy jaw. He usually had a permanent five o'clock shadow, but it was now starting to grow into a full beard. He didn't move. Emboldened, she ran her fingers down the length of his scar. It felt ridged. Hard. The damage had gone deep. A sword, perhaps?

His hair was loose, the black ribbon caught in the collar of his shirt. She drew it out and closed her hand around it. Nicholas murmured something she couldn't make out and then turned on his side, away from her.

Just as well. At this rate, in another moment she would have been stripping off his sweater. The thought made her flush, until she remembered what else might be keeping them company here during the night. The animal with the glowing eyes.

With a shudder she slipped out of the door and left Nicholas to his beauty nap.

Nicholas was traversing a series of tunnels. At first he thought he was underneath Blackfriars Abbey, back in the glory days of the Hellfire Club, but as he walked further into the darkness there was no sense of the familiarity that being under Lorne's family home should have brought to him.

He also felt very alone. His footsteps gave a dull echo and the ceiling was so low he was afraid he'd knock his head against it. When he rested a hand against the wall, it felt greasy. Water slid down and formed pools at his feet.

That was when he knew. He was in the between-worlds and dreams about that place never ended happily for him. He'd had plenty of them during the two hundred years he'd slept in Lorne's family mausoleum. They always seemed to start and end with him alone in a nasty tunnel.

He tried to tell himself that this was actually a good thing. He'd wanted to summon the Sorceress, and he knew she was here somewhere, lurking about. She always was. Well, he wasn't going to wander around like a lost soul until she decided she was ready to speak to him.

He needed to put a stop to this.

"I know you're there, madam!" His words echoed into a distance that seemed without end. "Can we cut this short? Surely we don't need to play these games anymore? I'm really no good at metaphors. Just tell me what you want."

"You can't expect to improve yourself unless you practice, Nicholas."

Her voice was right behind him. He jumped, but refused to spin around in haste and surprise. That was exactly what she wanted, to keep him off balance in every way possible. Instead, he gathered up his courage and turned slowly, arms folded, and met her eyes as if none of this frightened him. It was a lie, of course.

The Sorceress's red hair waved about her in a non-existent breeze and her eyes shone a brilliant blue. Her effect on him was tidal. She was the moon, and he was the ocean. Everything inside him was pulled out of shape so that he had to lean backwards slightly to keep from falling.

"Good morning, madam," he said in an even, polite

tone, when what he really wanted to do was turn and run. "What is it you require of me?"

A smile twitched on her mouth, and was gone in an instant. He hoped she wasn't in a playful mood—those times were always the worst.

"I wondered how you and Linny McNab were getting along together, Nicholas."

Again he tried not to show anything in his face, but this was the Sorceress. She could see through skin and blood and bone.

"I didn't realise we were meant to be 'getting along,'" he said with a dash of sarcasm.

She shook her head at him. The air crackled. "Stewart is still in the mortal world, plotting to destroy you and anyone else he can lay his hands on. And there is something else of concern. You know what I refer to, Nicholas, so don't play games. This isn't a contest between us, and if it was you could never win."

He sighed. "If you are eluding to the creature that Linny has brought back with her, then yes, madam, I know what you mean. In fact I had hoped to summon you in order to talk to you about that. What is it? What does it want? And how can we send it back to where it belongs?"

She looked thoughtful. "First we must discover why it has been set free," she said, and then laughed at the expression on his face. "I don't know everything, my lord. I'm flattered you believe I do."

"I'm not a lord," he retorted without thinking. "Not now."

"But you were," she reminded him, "and you could be again. The Earl of Northcote." She ran the title over her tongue and smiled her terrible smile. "You were a man of substance, once. A man to be reckoned with. You came from a long line of proud Darlingtons. But you threw it all away."

Nicholas grit his teeth. It did not do to tell the Sorceress to shut up. "I do not wish to discuss my past," he muttered.

She ignored him. "As for this creature that has slipped into the mortal world ... you're right, it has come from the place Linny McNab went. The place that Stewart sent her to after the Destroyer took her body."

"What does it want with her?"

"Questions that are yet to be answered."

He didn't like the smug look on her face, as if she knew something he didn't. But then he reminded himself that, while she did not know everything, she knew far more than he ever would. He'd been hoping she could fix things with a flick of her fingers or a bolt of lightning, but it was never that easy with the Sorceress. At best she was a guide, one who expected them to solve their own problems.

"What should I do?" he asked her. "Is there a way I can capture it so that I can keep it away from Linny?"

"That could be a problem. It seems very... attached to her."

"Any suggestions would be useful," he said, aware his desperation was showing.

The Sorceress smiled and it made his head ache. "You are very fond of your Scottish firebrand, aren't you? There may be hope for you yet, my lord."

He reined in his impatience. "At least tell me what it is, or where it has come from, madam. Maybe I can send it back in the same way Lorne sent the Destroyer back. With a spell."

The air crackled around her. "I fear it is not that simple," she said. "Have you heard of the Dark World, Nicholas?"

He hadn't, but it sounded suitably ominous.

"The Dark World belongs to me, but I do not have full control over what happens there. The Dark World is deep within my realm, where I send those I consider beyond my efforts at salvation. Those who need more robust treatment to reach redemption. If they fail the second time they go down into the underworld. In fact, the Dark World is so close to the underworld you can smell sulphur from its burning pits."

There was a sickness in his stomach, and a shakiness in his legs. Bad enough to have spent time in the between-worlds, but this Dark World sounded like a place he really did not want to visit.

"Is that where Linny was sent? The Dark World?"

"Yes, and the creature that has attached itself to your firebrand comes from that place. The creature has tethered itself to her. There is an open portal somewhere, allowing this connection to continue, and the only way to rid Linny McNab of her friend is break the tether that binds them and then close the portal. If that is not done, then I do not like her chances of survival, Nicholas."

"What does it want from her?" He knew he sounded shaken. The thought of Linny with that obscenity crouched over her made him want to smash something.

"I expect it wants to take her back to its realm. After that, who can say?" She raised her arms and her long sleeves danced in the silent winds that surrounded her.

"The demons of the Dark World are not mine to command. They lay outside the bounds of both my rule, and those of the underworld. I think you have Stewart to blame for this. He seeks to divide you and your friends. He is aware how fond you are of your Scot." She leaned closer and he felt his skull squeeze. "How much would you be willing to risk to save her, Nicholas?"

The light about her was pulsing. He couldn't have moved if he wanted to.

"Are you saying I have to go down to the Dark World?"

"Not a task for the faint hearted, I agree."

"But if that is the only way…"

She smiled her terrible smile. "Ah, I think you want to be a hero, Nicholas. You have made great strides toward redemption, and though you still have some way to go, I believe in you. Will you be a hero for your Linny?"

I am no hero, he wanted to say. I am the opposite of a hero. But before the words would form she had begun to fade. Next thing he knew he was standing all alone in that wretched tunnel.

Was entering the Dark World really the only option? A place next door to hell itself? He reminded himself that before the Sorceress sent him to sleep he had been in hell on earth so he should be used to it. What did it matter what happened to him? He couldn't bear the thought of Linny being lost to him forever, even if she wasn't truly his, not in the way he wanted her to be. A world without her in it was out of the question.

And if saving Linny McNab meant sacrificing himself, then so be it.

He needed to get back to Linny. Now. He needed to

tell her what he had discovered and what awaited her if that creature touched her. She would demand an explanation and he had to be ready to give it.

Nicholas stood in the tunnel and sighed. He knew the drill. The Sorceress wouldn't let him go easily. He'd have to wander about for a bit, go down some wrong turns, and become thoroughly lost, before she finally set him free from his dream.

She had told him once that it was to make a better man of him, although he wasn't quite sure how. He rather thought it was more to do with the witch's warped sense of humour. He comforted himself with the knowledge that she had at least given him some answers he could work with, no matter how unpleasant the solution.

Nicholas squared his shoulders and set off down into the dripping darkness.

Chapter Twelve

A IDEN SUTCLIFFE LOOKED UP FROM the sofa as Linny stepped out of the bedroom and closed the door behind her, leaving Nicholas to sleep.

The wide screen television was on, with lots of explosions and fake-sounding screams. Loki was lying at his feet. As the dog rose up and trotted over to her, his tail wagged.

Linny gave him a pat, grateful not to be knocked onto her back this time.

"Where's Maggie?" she asked.

Sutcliffe nodded toward the suite that her sister and Lorne shared. "Darlington is asleep?" he asked in his deep voice.

"Out like a light."

He smiled. With his handsome face, dark hair and eyes, combined with that tall, strong body, he was certainly an eye catching man. It wasn't just his looks though. There was an easy charm about him, slow to anger and quick to laugh. Linny wondered, if she hadn't met Nicholas, whether she might have been drawn to Aiden instead. He was certainly the more even-tempered of the three.

Too late.

Sometimes her inner voice annoyed the hell out of her.

Linny tried not to scowl as she walked across the thick, white carpet, despite enjoying the sensation on her bare feet. Was this how rich people lived their lives? She'd been too busy fretting about paying the next bill and getting Maggie everything she needed to worry about things like luxury. Maybe if they had been born to different parents things might have been different, but then she supposed she would have been another person, rendering the point moot.

She raised her hand to knock. At the last moment she hesitated and looked back at Sutcliffe.

"She *is* awake, Aiden?"

"Lorne took her breakfast in. Toast and black tea. Same as every morning." Sutcliffe lost interest and turned back to his game. Maggie had always been a cornflakes girl. Something about her sister's new breakfast of choice niggled at her and when she knocked quietly she was still trying to work out what it was.

Lorne opened the door. He looked less than impressed to see her, but then he always looked like that. Linny gave him her brightest smile, just to piss him off. "Maggie up?"

He glanced at Maggie to see if she had any objections, and then stepped back without a word and held open the door for her to enter.

"Thank you," she said cheerily.

Just one of the curtains was open and the view over Glasgow showed a city still in the early stages of waking up. Her eyes narrowed as she searched the room, and found her sister lying on the sofa, a slice of dry toast in one hand, and a grin on her pale lips.

"Hi," Maggie said. Then, when Linny's eyes narrowed even more, "You got me. I was going to tell you, but I wanted to wait and—"

"Oh God, you're pregnant." She couldn't help her voice sounding so flat when she said it. Her sister being pregnant was not something to rejoice. Not under these circumstances.

Maggie put down her toast. "You don't sound thrilled." She drew in a shaky breath. "Which is a pity, because Lorne and I are over the moon."

Lorne sat down beside her and took her hand in his, lifting it to his lips. "Definitely over the moon," he said, and looked into Maggie's eyes in a way that would have made a less feisty woman's heart melt.

"So, not an accident then," Linny said in a tone she knew did not help, but she couldn't seem to stop herself. It was achingly clear to her that this was not going to end well. Why on earth had they thought it was a good idea to have a baby when Lorne could be spirited back to the past at any moment? Of course, that was assuming he even survived the recapture of that maniac Stewart.

"Not an accident," Lorne answered. He gave Linny a frown, as if to warn her to tread carefully, then kissed Maggie's fingers again before he left the room. The door closed quietly behind him.

Maggie seemed to know there were going to be some hard questions, and took a moment to gather her strength. "Don't give me that look," she said, and set aside the half eaten toast with a grimace. "I know full well I could end up having this child on my own, but I'm prepared for that. I'm willing to take any risk."

Linny raised an eyebrow. "Are you? I raised you, remember? I know what it's like to be a single parent with very little support."

"I remember." Maggie struggled upright and for a moment appeared to be torn between staying put or making a run for the bathroom. Her eyes flickered to the door, but then the urge seemed to pass and she gave a sigh of relief. "And you did such a good job," she continued quietly. "I only hope I can do as good a job."

Linny tried to stop a smile. "You're trying to sweet talk me."

Maggie laughed. "Impossible."

"How far gone are you?" Her eyes slid down over her sister's slender body. There were signs of a baby bump. She remembered that the last time she had been with Maggie she had been wearing a baggy top, obviously to disguise the evidence. It hurt that Maggie hadn't told her straight away, but Linny also understood why her sister might be reluctant to share this piece of news.

"The baby's due in just under five months. Morning sickness seems to be lingering a lot longer than I thought it would."

Tears stung Linny's eyes and she blinked them away. No use letting Maggie see what a softy she really was. "You'll need my help," she said.

"I will. Lorne wanted me to tell you earlier … but I knew you'd be upset with me." Her dark eyes opened and they were bleak. "When this is all over, this might be the only thing I have left of him. The only thing to show that he was ever here in my world, and that we loved each other."

Linny came to sit beside her sister. "He's okay with this?"

"He is. We didn't make this decision lightly."

"You never do anything lightly," Linny retorted. Her sister tended to look at every problem sideways, upside down and downside up before she made a decision. Or at least, she had before Lorne came along.

Maggie took her hand. "So you'll be there for me? If I need you?"

Linny gave a shaky laugh. "You think I'm going to pass up the chance to be an auntie? But I warn you, I'll spoil this kid rotten."

Maggie smiled back, and wiped a tear from her cheek. "If it's are anything like Lorne, there can only be trouble ahead."

"Oh my God, a mini Marquis!"

Maggie chuckled. "We haven't told the others yet, but we'll have to soon. I was barely showing until recently, but I'm surprised they haven't noticed Lorne being even more attentive than usual. I'm so glad you're here with us now," she said. "We need to stay together. It's the only way we can be safe.

Stewart will do anything to divide us, Linny."

Linny squeezed her hand and took a deep breath. "Speaking of which, it's time I came clean as well."

Maggie's eyes popped. "You're not...?"

Linny made a noise in her nose. "Pregnant? Not likely. No, I need to tell you why I've been keeping my distance for so long."

Maggie listened in silence as she told the story. Linny skipped over some of the details, and toned down some of the worst bits, although she suspected her sister knew her too well to be fooled.

"*The Nightmare*," Maggie said once she had finished.

"The what?"

Maggie reached for her tablet and her fingers flew as she searched the internet. A moment later she laid the screen in front of them. "Is this it? There are several similar versions. You can see them all if you swipe."

Linny looked down and opened her mouth, but no sound came out. Adrenaline pumped through her and her hands shook.

On the screen was a painting of a bed and a woman sleeping, arms outflung, while a hideous creature squatted on top of her. There was something terribly vulnerable about the woman, as if she was under a spell, or in the midst of a dream. The squatting creature stared not at the woman, but the viewer. It was a close fit, but it wasn't the same as her demon. Then she turned to the next image, and the one after that, and took note of the differences in the artist's renderings.

Then she came across *the one*. Apelike, almost human but not quite, pointed ears and muscular, hairy shoulders. Apart from the lack of glowing eyes it was identical.

"Yes," she said at last, her voice raspy. "This, or a close cousin, at any rate. Where did you get this?"

Maggie gathered her thoughts. "This is a painting by Henry Fuseli dated 1781. It's called *The Nightmare*, and supposedly the subject, the woman, is in the throes of one, but there are also sexual connotations. It caused a bit of a scandal when it was first shown. The creature is said to represent an incubus, or a male demon, who, eh, preys upon sleeping women."

"Preys upon them in what way?" But even as she asked the question she already knew. An incubus was kind of like a male succubus, so… "Oh, wow, really?"

Maggie gave her a long look as she sought the right words to approach the subject. "Do you feel … have you…" She swallowed. "It hasn't *done* anything to you, has it?"

Linny stared back at her. "It hasn't got close enough to do anything."

Yet.

All this time she had been wondering what it wanted from her, why it tried to reach her every time she fell asleep, and why every cell in her body screamed at her to keep it from doing so. A sexual angle was not an answer she had considered and it turned her blood cold.

"Oh God." Maggie clutched her hand so tight

she felt her bones creak. "Have you really been dealing with this all on your own?"

"No. I mean, it didn't happen straight away. At first, after Blackfriars Abbey, there was just this uneasy feeling that something was wrong, but I didn't know what it was. At night I felt uneasy. I had trouble sleeping. Then I began to feel its presence in the room with me. I'd fall asleep and wake up suddenly, knowing something was there, watching. I didn't see it at first, only recently. As if it's gained strength over time, and now it's reached a point where it can appear to me. And *move*." She shuddered. "Maggie, I didn't want to tell you. I didn't want to bring *it* to *you*."

Maggie groaned with frustration. "But all on your own!"

"I wasn't completely on my own," she admitted. "Not recently, anyway. Nicholas knew something was wrong. Last night he went home with me and kept watch while I slept. As long as someone is awake then it won't come any closer, but at this point, if I fall asleep and there's no one around..." She put her hands over her face and pushed the screen with the disturbing painting away. "What am I going to do, Maggie?"

"What are *we* going to do," her sister countered. She considered the problem a moment. "Nicholas stayed up all night and kept watch? Where is he now?"

"Asleep."

"I suppose this can wait till he's had some rest."

Linny wanted to ask Maggie something about

Nicholas, but hesitated. Then the words were out of her mouth before she could stop herself. "What happened to his leg?"

Maggie picked up her tea, looked at it, then put it down again. "He doesn't talk about it and I haven't asked. If he's anything like Lorne, then he will tell you himself when he's ready. These men have been through hell and back, and they're proud of the changes they've made. Believe me, Linny, they're not who they once were. I've seen that for myself."

"Then why won't he talk about it?"

"Shame?" Maggie suggested. "Regret? Fear that you will think the worse of him if you learn the truth? Whatever it is, don't make the mistake of blaming the man he is for the man he once was."

Although Nicholas hadn't told her all of his secrets yet, he had met her halfway. It was Linny who had refused to let go of her fears long enough to give the two of them a chance.

Chapter Thirteen

L UNCH CONSISTED OF AN ARRAY of take-away boxes delivered to the penthouse. The five of them sat around the table, while Loki gave an occasional agonised moan as he watched.

Nicholas's deep sleep, rather than refreshing him, had made him groggy and disoriented. His visit with the Sorceress hadn't helped. Since he'd awoken in Lorne's family tomb, he tended not to sleep a great deal. It reminded him too much of the two hundred years he'd already slumbered through. He intended to make the most of his life, or what he had left of it, and sleep just seemed a waste of time.

He rubbed his hands over his face and pushed back his hair. He usually had it tied back, but after a fruitless search in the bedclothes for a ribbon, he'd left it loose. He could smell Linny's scent on the sheets, which had brought him semi erect with no way of relief, and that hadn't helped his mood. And now that she would sleeping with him more often, the situation was not about to change anytime soon.

He lusted after her, it was true, although she seemed determined not to give him a chance to show her how good such things could be between them. He wasn't sure why. Had this Keith villain she'd once known put her off anything resembling a relationship? Or was it seeing the mess her parents had made of their marriage? Perhaps Nicholas could tell her that his upbringing had also lacked in proper role models, and yet he was willing to try to achieve better.

He watched Linny take bites from the roti she'd been using to soak up the sauce from her meal as Maggie explained what they'd discovered about this *"Nightmare."* He followed that by recounting his conversation with the Sorceress. Now they were trying to absorb the information, and plan their next move.

Sutcliffe shoved a huge spoonful of lamb curry into his mouth. "So this thing, this demon, comes from the Dark World?"

"You can call it a demon but it's actually an incubus," Maggie said thoughtfully. She always seemed to be able to compartmentalise, pushing her emotion aside when necessary and see things with a cool and clear mind. On the other hand Linny was ruled by her emotions, which could make her irrational on occasion, but always passionate when it came to championing her beliefs.

Maggie's tablet lay in the centre of the table, and they had all viewed the painting. Darlington agreed it was very similar to what had stalked Linny in her bedroom. At first he had thought this was a step forward, but when he heard what the demon's possible motives were he had barely been able to restrain himself. He'd wanted to put his fist through the tablet, but chose instead to turn it over so that the incubus was hidden, saying it had ruined his appetite.

"Stewart must be behind it," Lorne said, his eyes like ice. "He's made a fool of the Sorceress. No wonder she wants him back, and no wonder he's doing everything he can to remain free."

"It's not about her," Maggie reminded him. "It's about you. Everything he does is about him and you. He's a single minded psychopath with abilities far beyond any human. Don't forget that."

Lorne reached out and took her hand in his. "I won't forget," he promised. "I have everything to lose if I do, and I'm not going to lose. Besides, the Hellfire Club has a few tricks of its own."

Had they, Nicholas thought? At least at Blackfriars Abbey they had been on familiar ground, while here they were a long way from their comfort zone. Nicholas didn't say so, however. He was aware of the reasons Lorne tried to play down the situation.

Linny spoke up, looking at Nicholas. "You said the Sorceress told you we have to go to the Dark World to stop the demon. Well, how do we do that? I mean, I don't suppose the Dark World shows up on Google Maps. We can't just punch in the GPS coordinates and get a roadmap."

Nicholas realised she had hoped he would have all the answers. He wished he did. The best he could do was, "If there's a portal, perhaps we can follow the demon back to its place of origin."

"Set Loki on to it?" Sutcliffe suggested, still eating.

"We don't know what it's capable of," Nicholas reminded them. "What if its power is on par with the Destroyer?"

Maggie shivered. No doubt she was remembering how the Destroyer had sucked the souls out of its innocent victims, including her sister. No, one wouldn't want to get too close to this new demon until they knew exactly what they were facing, and what it was capable of.

Maggie turned to him, her dark hair curling about her pale face. "If the Sorceress told you to go to the Dark World, then there must be a way of doing that. Can you call on her again, Nicholas?"

"I wish it were that simple. If she has a plan then she didn't share it with me. You know how devious she can be. No doubt she has something in mind, or several somethings. We may need to be patient until she reveals those plans to us."

"You're not the one with an incubus in the corner of your bedroom waiting to have his way with you," Linny muttered.

"Believe me, I am fully aware of how dangerous the situation is," he retorted with a growl in his voice. The thought of anything or anyone touching Linny McNab against her will made his blood boil.

"*Are* you?" she said, that snarky note returning to her voice. "I feel like I'm some sort of toy in a game I want no part in. Stewart hates Lorne, so he's using the rest of us to try to get at him. He's set this demon on me to unsettle the rest of you. I was right, wasn't I, Nicholas? I told you I should stay away. I told you I was contaminated."

There was an outcry, but Nicholas spoke over the noise. "And I told you that was nonsense. We're all in this together. What do you think would happen if you were carried off to the Dark World?"

They glared at each other. Everyone else had fallen silent.

"You could all get on with your lives?" Linny's voice had turned shaky, and he could read the fear in her eyes. As usual, her anger had been all about hiding that fear.

He leaned close. "No. I would follow you down there, and I wouldn't come back until I'd found you. Now, will you stop playing the martyr?"

She stared at him a moment and then suddenly she was on her feet. The chair fell to the floor behind her, and she set off at a run toward the bedroom.

"Hell," he muttered, and followed her as fast as his lame leg would allow him to.

Behind him, he heard Maggie start to get up, and then Lorne say, "Wait. Let Nicholas deal with this."

Linny had slammed the door so hard that it had swung open again. Instead of bursting in after her he took a calming breath before he entered. She stood with her back to him, eyes focused on the narrow window.

The view here wasn't spectacular like the one from Lorne's suite, but she wasn't looking at it anyway. Her reflection was visible against the grey sky and he could tell she was crying.

Nicholas closed the door behind him and came up behind her. Her shoulders stiffened but she neither spoke nor moved. Darlington put his arms around her and pulled her back against the shelter of his body.

Just for a moment she held herself back, and then crumpled into him. She turned around into his arms, her face jammed against his chest, and her hands in fists against his shirt. He felt her shake as sobs were forced out of her. He said nothing, just held her, and let the emotion drain out of her. She was so determined not to be a burden on Maggie and the rest of them, but that had taken its toll. She couldn't see that their strength was in staying together. Showing a united front. It was only when Stewart managed to separate them that he came close to success. And even then they had risen to the occasion.

When Linny had been taken by the Destroyer, they had moved heaven and earth to get her back, despite having to release Stewart in the process. Now she was here and Nicholas wasn't going to let anything happen to her again.

Eventually she grew quiet against him. He smoothed back her silky hair, and then cupped her cheeks, lifting her face toward his.

"Don't," she said in a husky voice, and tried to pull away. "I'm a wreck."

But he wouldn't allow her to hide again. He bent his head and kissed her gently on her soft, trembling mouth. She gasped and he felt her hands creep up over his shoulders and around his neck, holding on.

"You can't keep trying to save me, Nicholas," she whispered.

"Of course I can," he whispered, nuzzling her hair. When he found the warm skin of her neck, he pressed his lips there. His voice sounded more vulnerable than he'd have preferred but that was because he was being honest. "Because I want you to save me, too. I think we can save each other."

"So many reasons why that should be a hard no," she groaned.

"Unless the yeses outweigh the noes."

She chuckled, her fingers now tangled in his hair. "You don't give up, do you?"

"I've had two hundred years to perfect my obstinacy."

"And you always have to have the last word, too."

"Linny…"

"I'm not good at … *this*." She waved a hand between the two of them. "I don't want to hurt you. I feel like I will."

"We need to practice," he said. "We need to talk. There are things you need to know, and afterwards it may be me who hurts you."

"Maggie said she saw what you were like back in your own time, and that none of you are the men now that you were back then. She said I should remember that."

He closed his eyes and rested his forehead against hers. "I have not been a good man, Linny."

"Aren't bad men capable of changing?"

"There are some things I doubt can ever be forgiven."

He could see she wanted to ask him what he
had done that had been so unforgivable. The words
trembled on her lips. Linny was worried she would
hurt him but he knew in his heart that he was
going to be the one to hurt her. Then she would
hate him and there would be nothing he could do
about it. This, whatever this was, would be over.

So, like a coward, he was relieved when Lorne
called for them from the other room. That meant
he didn't have to tell her just yet. Another minute,
another hour, another day before she had reason to
hate him, and he was happy to take the reprieve.

Nicholas took Linny's hand in his and held it
tight.

"This isn't done," he promised as they left the
room. "Not nearly done."

Chapter Fourteen

———

THE TELEVISION WAS ON AND everyone was on their feet, the meal forgotten, gathered around the big screen.

"What—?" Nicholas began, only to be shushed. Linny felt light headed. A moment ago they had been on the verge of *something* together. Now they were back in the maelstrom that was life with the Hellfire Club.

Nicholas pulled her over behind Lorne—he still had hold of her hand. The news anchor had finished talking and now the scene changed to a field reporter on the scene, a young man in a woollen coat with his hair brushed fashionably to one side.

"I'm here in Port Finlay, but so far no one has any answers. Word came in earlier this morning that the town is empty. Completely empty. Everyone appears to have just *vanished*." The reporter wasn't sure what else to say. Voices were raised behind him, and suddenly an army truck rolled into view. The camera panned around the scene. The town did look deserted, apart from men in uniform gathered in a group, as they listened to an officer give commands.

"Port Finlay," Maggie said suddenly. "We had a place there. Simon and I. A holiday cottage."

Before Lorne could respond, the broadcast reclaimed their attention.

"How did we come to learn about this?" the studio anchor asked.

The young reporter blinked. "A young man had booked out the local pub for a wedding party but when he arrived to get started on preparations he found there was no one there. At first he assumed the pub hadn't opened, but he soon realized none of the local stores were open and nobody was on the streets. At first he thought there might been an evacuation, a possible gas leak, but when he couldn't find any notifications or police barricades, he went looking."

"And he didn't find anyone?" the studio anchor asked.

"Nobody. He soon called the police, and when he learned there hadn't been an evacuation, asked them to send someone to investigate." The reporter then waved to the army truck, and soldiers setting up a barricade. "That eventually lead to what you see here now. It's like the Mary Celeste. Reports are coming in of meals served up but uneaten, coffee cups sitting on tables in front of televisions that were left on, but the people are gone. Just … gone."

"Could it be some kind of hoax?" the studio anchor asked. "A community prank?"

"Some people have speculated it to be some

kind of 'flash mob' kind of stunt intended for social media, but that seems unlikely given the circumstances."

"What do the police say?"

"They're baffled. Completely baffled."

"And the army? What's their position?"

The reporter swallowed. "They have no comment at this time; they are simply securing the town. I'm about to get moved on. They have, however, called in an expert. I'll try to talk with him before he crosses the barricade."

A moment later they were back in the television studio, where there were a half-dozen guests ready to give their opinions. Linny looked around at the penthouse and knew they didn't need any experts. They already knew what had happened.

"Stewart," Lorne said, his voice soft with menace. "Only he could do something like this. He's sending us a message. He wants us to follow him to Port Finlay."

"Why there?" Sutcliffe demanded, jaw clenched, arms folded, while Loki sat anxiously at his feet.

"I'm sure when we get there we'll find out."

Maggie pressed against Lorne, who put his arm around her. Linny put her hand on Nicholas's arm and he seemed instantly aware of her. He bent his head.

"Are we really going to go after Stewart just because he's giving us his middle finger?" she asked, in a voice too low for Maggie to hear.

"Our task is to capture him," he reminded her.

"But he knows that. It's obviously a trap."

His brown eyes stared into hers as he read her. He'd already learned her snarkiness and sometimes her temper were just a front to hide her fear. The Linny McNab behind the smart mouth and blunt utterances was, more often than not, afraid.

She thought he might call her on it, but instead he spoke in a rational tone. "Of course. But you forget, we're not completely helpless. We have the Sorceress on our side."

She gave a shudder. "Fat lot of good she's been so far."

"It seems pointless to me," said Sutcliffe, arms crossed and still frowning at the screen. "There are any number of ways he could get our intention. Why this?"

"He has to take everything that belonged to Simon," Maggie said. Her voice had a tremble in it. "Stewart is stealing his identity all over again. There's more to this than just sending you a message."

"Regardless of his motives, we'll stop him," Lorne said with confidence. "He's arrogant and thinks himself invincible. This may be our best chance to confront and contain him before he does any more damage."

Maggie took a breath to steady herself, to force back the emotions that were starting to surface. "You're right," she agreed. "Maybe this will be the mistake we've been waiting for him to make."

"But what about all the people in the town?" Linny asked, one eye still on the television. "How many lived there?"

"I think about a hundred and fifty," Maggie said. "I know what you're asking. Where are they?"

Sutcliffe rubbed his unshaven jaw. "It's possible they could have been transported to another time. Or perhaps set outside of time altogether. I assume Stewart's powerful enough to do that."

Nicholas stared at the screen, but his thoughts seemed elsewhere. "What about the Dark World?" He looked around at the others. "According to the Sorceress it lies outside her power. It could be part of this game he's playing, to do that right under the Sorceress's nose. Show her up, make her feel as if he's her master."

"If that's the case, then I'm guessing our witchy friend will have a vested interest in backing us up," Linny said. "She'll want to bring him down, and we're her best chance of making that happen. We should use that to our advantage."

Nicholas looked at her and smiled. And it was only then that she realised that she had said "we." Linny had declared herself to be part of the team.

They took two cars, one for Maggie and Lorne, and the other with Sutcliffe and Loki in the back, and Linny and Nicholas in the front. When Nicholas announced his intention to drive there was a loud cry of "No!" from Sutcliffe and a howl from Loki. Linny put her hands over her ears but she was laughing.

"Is he so terrible?" she asked, taking the driver's

seat.

"Maggie tried to teach him, but she stopped when we ended up in a field for the fourth time," he said. "Nicholas has no understanding of modern mechanics. He treats it like a curricle."

Linny grinned. "I can just imagine."

"You're no better," Nicholas grumbled, clicking in his passenger side seat belt.

"At least I do not pretend to be," his friend retorted, as laid back as always. "I accept my limitations."

Linny joined the stream of traffic headed north, keeping the other car in sight and thinking about her passengers. The three men were so different, she wondered how they had become friends. Outcasts finding comfort with other outcasts? Perhaps.

No one was sure how long they'd be in Port Finlay, so they'd taken enough luggage to last a week, and left the remainder at the penthouse.

As they drove northward the traffic began to thin out. Port Finlay was off the main motorway, along a winding stretch of secondary road with a backdrop of mountains and sea lochs. Linny had stayed at Maggie and Simon's cottage once and that had been enough for her. The isolation was uncomfortable for one so used to city living. The thought that she could sit on the rocks and not see another soul for hours wasn't one she liked to dwell on. Crowds meant safety.

Linny still wasn't sure this was a good idea. How did they even know Stewart would be waiting for them? And if he was, how would they put the Sorceress's ring on his finger? How did they know he hadn't set up a trap? There were still far too many unanswered questions for her liking.

Sutcliffe spoke up and put an end to her musings. "Do you ever miss the past?" he asked Nicholas. "I mean the sheer selfishness of drinking in the crypt all night and then sleeping the day away."

Even without turning her head she felt Nicholas's eyes on her—and yes, there was a time when she would have said that was impossible. He was probably wondering how best to answer with consideration to her feelings. His concern was no longer surprising and unexpected, but she still hadn't figured out how to deal with it. Very few men in her life had been concerned for her lack of well-being; in fact most of them had been the main cause of it. Her father had been an abusive arsehole and Keith, although claiming to love her, turned nasty whenever things didn't go his way.

Nicholas had punched Keith when he tried to hurt her. Then he had come home with her and sat up all night, just so she could sleep. Such selflessness was confusing and at the same time pretty damn wonderful. Linny wasn't sure what to make of it, apart from jumping his bones and having a sex marathon with him. Maybe it would come to that. She wasn't sure how much longer she could resist him, despite knowing that he expected a lot more of her than a one night stand.

From Regency rake to monogamous rake, if there was such thing. It made her want to smile. She had accepted that she was infatuated with him, but she feared she was becoming obsessed.

"Not in that way," Nicholas finally answered.

"In what way do you miss it then?" Sutcliffe asked.

"Just the three of us being together. Good company, even if we were doing bad things."

"How did you all meet?" Linny asked, following up on her thoughts from a moment ago.

"At a club in town," Sutcliffe said.

"You mean like White's?" Linny had read her share of Regency romances. "Or … what was the other one?"

"Brooks'," Nicholas said promptly. "My father put my name down there when I was born. Took it off again. But to answer your question, no, not a gentleman's club. This was the sort of club that hides in the back alleys, where bored men with too much time on their hands drink and dally. One night, after we'd all imbibed far too much, Lorne told us we were going to form the Hellfire Club and he had just the place for it. We agreed to join him immediately."

"And what about now? Do you miss the drink and the dallying?" She tried not to sound judgemental. Besides, she had no right to judge anyone. She had done plenty of stupid things in her life too, though none quite as stupid as setting a malevolent supernatural force loose on the English countryside.

"Definitely not," Nicholas answered promptly, and Aiden murmured his assent. "We have been shown the error of our ways. Or perhaps it would be more accurate to say that the Sorceress taught us to look more closely at those ways, and instead of perpetuating our mistakes or wallow in regret over those mistakes, to accept them and move on."

"And have you? Accepted your mistakes?"

Silence. Aiden answered from the back seat when it was obvious Nicholas wasn't going to. "It is an ongoing process."

Linny wanted to probe further but she knew when to let something go, for now at least.

"I thought the Sorceress was just a scary witch woman, but maybe there's a bit of therapist in there somewhere," she said, with a glance at Nicholas. Her hands tightened on the wheel. "Not that she tried to improve my personality. She just scared the hell out of me. Why did she choose the three of you to play her mind altering games on?"

Nicholas ran a hand over his face, tracing the line of his scar in a way that was obviously habit. Reminding himself of the past, perhaps? "In the beginning I thought it was simply punishment, but as time went on I began to understand that she genuinely wanted me to see for myself that I could be a better man. I'm not sure if that means she has a heart … sometimes I'm sure she hasn't. When she takes me to the between-worlds I wonder if she's ever going to let me go, or just leave me to wander those tunnels forever. She isn't kind, Linny."

"The tunnels? You too?" Sutcliffe growled. "I thought it was just me. That place is a never ending nightmare, and I really think I would do anything to get out of it."

"So she's changed you both through fear?" Linny said, even more curious now. The between-worlds did sound like a nightmare. She wondered uncomfortably whether, if the threat of it was ever removed, the three men would slip back into their old ways.

Aiden and Nicholas locked eyes in the rear view mirror.

"Not fear," Aiden answered her. "At first, maybe it played a part, but in time that became a genuine desire to be a better man."

Nicholas cleared his throat and looked embarrassed. "And the realisation that we could. Be better, I mean. That anything was possible." It seemed that even after two hundred years, talking about feelings was awkward for these men.

"It still sounds a bit like brainwashing," Linny said.

"The Sorceress reminded me of what I once was and what I am striving to become." Nicholas's voice was serious as he leaned slightly toward her. Then, with a shallow breath, he added, "The gap between the two is still vast. I am not a good man, Linny. I accept that. But I am still learning, even if it takes a lifetime."

She gave him a frown. "Even good men can do bad things," she reminded him, but her heart rate had picked up, and her skin prickled beneath the intensity of his stare. "I mean, how bad could you have been?"

She could tell he was considering not answering her. She wouldn't have been surprised if he made some excuse—she didn't like discussing her deepest, darkest secrets either. But finally he answered.

"I killed someone. Through my own negligence I took life."

"Nicholas," she whispered.

"Not through anger or vengeance, nor anything that could justify what I did. I was too busy thinking about myself and what mattered to me. I deserved this." He pointed to the scar on his cheek. "I deserve everything that has happened to me. I needed to suffer and I have, but it still isn't enough."

She didn't know what to say and before she could find the words, Aiden cleared his throat. "He's right. We're not good men. We're not being punished unfairly, Linny. And yet I do not believe we are intrinsically evil. If we were, then, like Stewart, we would not have been given a chance to redeem ourselves. The Sorceress saw good within us, and I'm grateful for that."

She had never heard Aiden talk like that before. He always seemed to take each moment as it came, refusing to allow himself to become too serious or reflective about anything. Right now he was deadly serious.

Linny turned her attention back to the road, but her mind was still dwelling on their past. The Hellfire Club. She'd heard the story. In the beginning it had sounded ridiculously tame to her, no worse than the back pubs of Glasgow on a Saturday night. But Maggie had assured her it wasn't. Her sister had seen them as they once were with her own eyes, and Maggie wasn't one to make things up.

Nicholas stared out the window, jaw rigid. She knew she had got as much soul searching as she was going to get from him and Aiden for a while. Would he tell her more eventually? He'd said he would. The thing was, she was no longer so sure she wanted to know.

On the other hand, Nicholas was determined to keep her safe. He seemed to genuinely care about her. And she desired him in a way she had never desired another man before. She just wasn't sure if that was enough for them to be totally honest with each other.

───◆───

The further they drove along the Scottish coast, the more spectacular the views became. Misty islands rose out of a sea of restless waves and darting seabirds. This landscape was foreign to Nicholas, and yet it touched something inside him. Perhaps it was the loneliness. There were times when he had felt so alone in his own life, even in the midst of a crowd. The scenery might be beautiful, but there was also a terribleness about it that reminded him of the Sorceress.

Darlington had been brought up in the gentle green countryside of Oxfordshire, on his family estate, apart from the time spent away at school. He'd been bored. The road ahead of him seemed to be already marked out, his life structured. Tame. He'd longed for something different and exciting, and that had led him into trouble.

Matters only escalated from there.

By the time his parents had sent him to Italy they were ready to wash their hands of him. After all, they had a perfectly good replacement in his brother. By the time he came home again, barely alive, the decision had been made. He was disinherited and stripped of his title. There was nothing to do but spend his days in debauchery. Because that was all he believed he was good for.

When Loki started whining Linny stopped the car and climbed out. He joined her, and Aiden took Loki out to do his thing. The wind felt fresh and sharp against Nicholas's face. He watched Linny huddle deeper into her black coat, her fair hair tucked into the collar. She'd fallen silent after their conversation and he wondered if she was already regretting her curiosity about his past.

He limped to the edge of the nearby cliff. A few feet from his shoes the world dropped away into a fury of broken rock and boiling water. His dark hair was loose—he still hadn't found his ribbon— and the salty gusts whipped the strands about his face.

He sensed Linny was watching him. If he turned to face her now, what would he see? Desire or fear? Need or rejection? Earlier today, he'd told her that if they were honest with each other, if they talked, then maybe they could see their way clear to calm waters. But what future was there between the two of them? He was on a mission to capture a demon and save the world, and afterwards he might still be returned to the past with Lorne to pay the price for their reckless behaviour.

A seabird screamed, hovering above them on the updraft. He started and looked up.

"Is that you, Sorceress?" Sutcliffe called out back by the car. "Are you watching over us?" His cries went unanswered. He shook his head and opened the car door for Loki. "Are we going, or are you planning to go for a swim?" he shouted to Darlington, sounding uncharacteristically unsettled.

As Nicholas moved to join him, he saw that Linny was still watching him. For a moment neither of them looked away. They were trapped in a situation that in all likelihood would end badly. And yet selfishly he still wanted to take the risk. Even if they had but one day together.

Chapter Fifteen

———◆———

THE LITTLE TOWN OF PORT Finlay was lit up with blue and orange flashing lights. Police cars and army trucks blocked the road when they reached the entry point, and Linny had no choice but to stop her car behind Maggie's. A soldier came to the open window to speak to her sister and Lorne, and she wondered whether they would be told to turn back. Or arrested.

To her surprise, Lorne got out of the car and stood a moment, talking with the man, and then he looked back and gave a nod. It appeared this was the signal for Aiden and Nicholas to join him, and Linny had no intention of waiting in the car alone.

It was chillier than she expected, and Linny reached for her coat. She wound her scarf around her neck as she joined the group, but before she reached them Maggie pulled her aside.

"They were expecting us," she said.

"What do you mean? The police?"

Maggie nodded, her face white and strained,

which set off all of her sister's protective instincts. "They said that a colleague of the late Professor Simon Frazer, a Doctor Noakes, has been waiting to speak to us."

Linny took her hand, squeezing her fingers hard. "Then it *isn't* Stewart," she breathed with relief.

"Oh it is. Noakes was his mother's name. She was also Lorne's nanny. Stewart is reminding us what this is all about."

"Their past?"

"Noakes is here *advising* the authorities," she went on in a stilted voice that tried to be emotionless.

"About what? Is he supposed to be a Professor of Missing Villagers or something?"

"I don't know how or why. He could have talked them into believing his presence was necessary. But he's in there, and he is expecting us."

"You don't have to go in there—" Linny began, wanting nothing more than to hustle her sister back into her car and drive her to safety.

"Of course she doesn't," Lorne said. The man was right behind them, his icy blue eyes full of disquiet. "I told her not to come. Perhaps she'll listen to you."

For the first time since she'd met him, the two of them were in perfect accord.

"I want to be here," Maggie said with a flash of temper. "I *need* to be here. Do I really have to explain myself to you again?"

Lorne closed his eyes and Linny could almost see him counting to ten. When he opened them, the apprehension had been replaced by a warmth she rarely saw, apart from when he looked at Maggie. "My love…" he began.

There was a squawk from the radio on the soldier's belt. They all waited as he answered it. He abruptly stopped, found Lorne, and stepped forward to hand it over. "He's on the other end," he said, taking a step back.

"Doctor Noakes, what a pleasure," Lorne said dryly.

"Ah, Marquis, so good of you to drop by, old boy."

Linny felt a moment of disorientation and then fury. Same old Stewart, everything was a joke to him, wearing different bodies like they were Halloween costumes. She heard that distinctive throat clearing that had given him away last time he pretended to be someone else.

"How are things?" he asked cheerfully.

"Come and face me and I'll tell you."

"I don't think that's wise, Marquis. I'm here to help the authorities with this little problem. Fancy losing a whole village!"

"And how can *you* help?" Lorne said, cutting through Stewart's chuckle. "Why did they mention Professor Simon Frazer?"

"It seems there is a legend in Port Finlay that back in the day, as in a couple of hundred years ago, everyone vanished. I might or might not have had something to do with that, but I'm not admitting guilt. Anyway, that it's happened again seems a bit too much of a coincidence, and because I was researching a new book, in collaboration with Professor Frazer, about this very incident, they have asked me for my help."

"Despite the fact that this is all a pack of lies? I thought this was the future. Shouldn't it be a simple matter for them to confirm who you really are—or aren't in this case?"

"Ah well, I might have thrown a bit of magic about. A bit of glamour. Let people see what they want to see. And you know, Marquis, I find if you talk with enough authority people tend to believe you. You should know that. You've been deceiving people for your own advantage for centuries."

"You sound a bit peeved," Lorne said. "Still jealous that your mother loved me best?"

Silence.

"Come out and face me," Lorne said softly, his hand tightening on the device. "Let's end this now."

When Stewart spoke again, it was with a suppressed note of excitement. "Is Linny there? I wanted a little word with her."

Lorne shot her a questioning glance. When she nodded he held out the device and she took it, her fingers feeling cold and stiff despite her gloves.

"What is it, freak?"

Stewart chuckled in delight. "Oh, I love her," he declared. "No pretending to be polite, just pure unadulterated loathing. How is your little midnight friend, Linny?"

Linny's breath stuttered. He *knew*. Well, of course he did! He must have known all along. Probably even planned it.

She was just about to tell him what she thought of him when Nicholas stepped in and shook his head, warning her to be calm and careful. Behind him the soldier watched on with a frown although he was out of earshot.

Linny fought back her urge to verbally abuse the man who had caused so much pain. "Perhaps you could be a dear and tell me how to send my little friend home," she said, feigning politeness. "I'm tired of him now and you've had your fun."

"I'm sure you are tired," Stewart sounded gleeful. "But I'm afraid he won't want to go willingly. The only way to make him is to return him to where he came from yourself. You're going to enjoy taking him home."

"The Dark World?" she said, against her better judgement, her eyes still on Nicholas's.

"Ah, so you know something of it." Stewart said, and despite the hint of amusement in his voice he sounded deadly serious. "Yes. It's the only way,"

"You bastard," she hissed.

That laugh again, and then Lorne took the device back. "Come out and face us," he said furiously. "Face *me*, you coward."

"Coward?" Evidently Stewart needed to have the last word. "Perhaps I'm just playing the long game, Marquis."

And then he was gone. Lorne handed the radio back to the soldier. The man's expression was confused, and Linny wondered if he even understood what they were saying—perhaps part of Stewart's abilities was 'scrambling' conversations for those not involved.

"Can we enter the village?" Maggie asked, turning to the soldier. "We'd like to see Doctor Noakes. As you know, he and my husband were colleagues and I have some important information regarding the book they were writing."

Lorne's jaw tightened but he said nothing.

"I'll have to ask for orders. Wait here." The soldier turned and left to find a superior officer.

"Lorne, give me the ring. He won't be expecting me to approach him. He won't know what's happening until it's too late."

Lorne appeared horrified by the suggestion. "Maggie—"

"Maggie, are you crazy?" Linny hissed. "You can't go in there. That's what he wants. If you go in to see him—"

"What else can we do?" she said, arms folded around herself. "He's here, we're here. It's our chance. Lorne?"

"There is no way I am allowing you to get close to that creature." Lorne looked more agitated than Linny had ever seen him.

"He will be ready for you," Nicholas said. "Maggie, he's playing games, just as he did at the Abbey. Lorne's right."

"Stewart's motives are rarely what they appear to be. There is always another angle involved," Sutcliffe spoke up.

"Do you ever get the feeling you're being manipulated?" Nicholas grumbled.

"All the time," said Lorne.

But Maggie had gone beyond the limits of her patience. "Will you just give me the ring?" she demanded, and held out her hand. Lorne made no move to obey her and Linny was grateful for that.

"Maggie," she sighed.

"I just want it to be over," her sister said in a shaky voice. "I just want that evil man gone."

"We all want that, but not if it puts your life at risk!" Lorne had reached his limit too.

The soldier was back. "You are allowed in, madam," he said to Maggie, "but no one else."

Linny and Lorne both objected, loudly, but Maggie took off before they could stop her. When they tried to follow, a pair of soldiers moved in to force them back. Then there was a flash of grey fur, and Loki was running after her. There was no stopping him.

Linny screamed for her sister to come back, but the cry was drowned out by a tremendous explosion.

Chapter Sixteen

T HERE WAS A SOUND. A door closing.
Linny tried to open her eyes but they seemed
to be fused shut. Panic ramped up within her and
she struggled to sit up, scratching at her face as if
she could tear her eyes open through sheer force.

"No." A pair of arms wrapped around her, their
strong hold hampering her efforts to pry open
her eyes. His warm breath brushed against her ear.
Nicholas. "Wait. Just wait. You must have landed
face first in the mud when the explosion went off."

"Here." Another male voice, this one unfamiliar.

Before she could get any answers, something cool
stroked over her face, and then her closed eyelids. A
cloth soaked in warm water. Linny sat, trembling,
trying not to panic. Nicholas was murmuring to
her about everything being all right and that he
was there and in a moment she would see where
she was. Beneath her she could feel a hard bench
and there was a smell.

Ashes. Burning. From the explosion? Something
stung her nostrils, making her heart rate pick up

even though she didn't know why. The smell of burnt matches.

Sulphur.

"You should be able to open your eyes now." Nicholas held her chin with a firm hand, turning her face this way and that as if to admire his hand-iwork.

Cautiously, Linny opened them. The world was blurry and dark, but as she blinked quickly things began to come back into focus. They were inside a building, and a distant ceiling rose into the shadows above. It looked like a medieval hall. Her confused thoughts ran in circles. Had the army brought them to an old cathedral after the explosion? Or was it a castle?

And then she remembered who had been near that explosion.

"Maggie!"

Nicholas stepped in front of her, a smear of mud on his cheek, his forehead creased into a worried frown. "Linny, listen to me," he said sharply. "*Listen!*"

He held her back as she twisted in his arms, trying to get away. To find Maggie. Then she noticed a small man standing nearby, watching them. His face was as round as a ball and, bizarrely, he was dressed like a medieval jester, complete with shoes that were so long at the toe that they had to be tied to his knees with fancy ribbons.

Linny blinked, completely confused. "What the f—?"

Nicholas squeezed her hand to regain her attention. "This is Zany," he said with a nod at the jester. "And we are in the Dark World."

"*The* Dark World?" She didn't want to believe him.

"The same."

Linny looked about her more carefully this time. The lack of light meant that sharp lines melted and merged with the background. It seemed as if the place went on forever.

"But how?" she breathed.

Nicholas ran his thumb back and forth over the raised seam of his scar. "I don't know," he admitted. "I awoke on the ground outside and he was shaking me," with a nod at Zany. "I carried you inside and the doors slammed shut behind us. That's what woke you up."

She heard him and yet it was as if his words were sliding off her, the meaning of them eluding her. Her brain was still back in Port Finlay and the explosion had just gone off.

Maggie?" she said again, a whisper now.

His eyes softened in sympathy. "I don't know, Linny. I'm sorry."

Her gaze slid past his and saw that this person he'd called Zany was still watching them, his expression one of sly curiosity. The little man was deformed, one shoulder higher than the other, and one of his legs was shorter, so that when he moved he seemed to be bouncing. If she was feeling more herself she might have made an Igor joke.

"We have not had any visitors here for a long time," he said, with a crafty upward glance, and then sniggered as if *he*'d made a joke. "Those who are residents don't expect to be visited. They are here because it is their last chance to find redemption." His face sobered, his eyes seeming to look inward. "Best you have nothing to do with any of them."

Linny tried not to let him frighten her. She had to get out of here, that was the important thing. She had to find Maggie and make sure she was all right.

But something in Nicholas's expression had her heart hammering. The fog in her brain began to clear and she remembered. Stewart's jeering words prior to the explosion.

The Dark World, Linny. You've been there before. You're going to enjoy taking him home.

"The demon from the painting," she said, her voice rising in pitch. "It came from here. Stewart did this. This is one of his tricks. He sent us here, didn't he? He—"

Nicholas cut her short. "I don't know, Linny. I wish I did."

She wrapped her arms around herself, shivering. This was all Stewart, it had to be. He would do anything to see his enemy destroyed. Cause havoc and heartbreak, whatever collateral damage was needed, just to bring Lorne down. But this wasn't about death, Stewart didn't want to just kill Lorne. He wanted him broken.

"You are chilled. Come and warm yourself."

They turned at the interruption. She'd forgotten about Zany. The little man had begun his uneven, bouncing walk down the vast hall. Looking beyond him she caught her first glimpse of the flaring torches that fought the darkness. At the very end of the hall was an enormous hearth with roaring flames.

"You *are* chilled," Nicholas said, taking her cold hand in his warm one. His touch was comforting and instinctively she clung a little tighter. "We may as well be comfortable while we consider how to extract ourselves from our current situation."

"Our current situation?" His sangfroid made her giggle, but she covered her mouth before it could turn into full blown nervous hysteria. "You sound as if this is an everyday event for you."

He gave her a frown, brows drawn down at the middle, as if he didn't know what she was amused about. "I've been through worse."

Well that was true enough. Her desire to laugh left her. Suddenly she was very glad he was here with her because if anyone could get them out of The Dark World, it was Nicholas Darlington.

Hand in hand they followed Zany, Nicholas limping at her side. Where was his cane? She was tempted to offer her arm for support, but she wasn't sure how he would take that. He tended to be touchy when it came to his infirmity.

Soon enough, the heat of the massive medieval fireplace became evident. Linny felt its warmth on her face with an almost painful intensity.

The Dark World? Was this really where they were? It looked more like a medieval castle, or one of those ancient long houses Maggie used to bang on about.

Not *used to*, she corrected herself. Maggie wasn't dead. Maggie couldn't be dead...

She bit her lip, hard, and took a shaky breath. To distract herself, she tried to remember if Stewart had been speaking the truth. Was it here she'd been tucked away, while the Destroyer invaded her body? She had vague recollections, but they were brief, flickering images. A tunnel, she'd thought at the time, the sort of thing that the others had described when they spoke of the between-worlds. But according to Stewart she hadn't been in there. Maybe all of these vile places looked the same.

Nicholas squeezed her hand, and she realised she'd missed something. "Sorry?"

"The Dark Lord will be here soon," Zany repeated. His gaze shifted from Linny to Nicholas. "He won't be happy to see strangers in his hall. Not when they weren't invited."

"The Dark Lord?" Linny whispered. She was completely out of her depth. Perhaps the explosion had knocked her unconscious and this was just a dream? Yet Nicholas's hand in hers was strong and warm, and so very real. It didn't feel like she was asleep and nothing was quite that simple in her life.

"He rules this place," Zany told them over his shoulder. "The Dark World is part of the Sorceress's domain, but she does not rule it. Those souls she thinks are worth saving she keeps to herself, those she wishes she could save but cannot, she sends down here. The ones beyond redemption go straight to the underworld."

"So this isn't hell?" Linny asked.

"No, but sometimes you can smell it." Zany bounded up to a huge chair set upon a dais near the fireplace and quickly climbed up onto it, grinning as he made himself comfortable. "Not many people know we're even here. The Sorceress keeps it a secret. That's why we don't get many visitors."

"Why does she keep it a secret?" Linny asked, as she moved closer to the intense fire.

"The Lords of the Universe wouldn't approve. They don't like her saving souls as it is, and they certainly wouldn't like to think she was stashing those she thinks worthy of a second chance down here. By rights they should go straight to hell." He smirked at the expression on her face. "You're a mortal, aren't you?"

"What's wrong with being a mortal?" she snapped. "And for your information I have been down here before. I just … don't remember it all that well."

He gave her a curious look.

Linny didn't want him to ask her questions. Not just because her head ached, but because she had no real answers. For instance, if she and Nicholas were here, then where was Maggie?

The huge doors at the far end of the hall swung open and crashed shut again. Linny spun around, eyes wide, breath catching in her throat. For a moment there was silence, and then footsteps echoed, coming closer. Heavy footsteps that seemed to rock the building.

Zany scrambled off the chair, moving respectfully to its side as he peered through the gloom. "My lord is coming," he announced in a foreboding way that Linny was sure was meant to scare her. He succeeded.

She felt Nicholas's hand gripping hers again. Maybe he had never let it go. The footfalls came closer and out of the shadows loomed a man. Linny wasn't sure what she had been expecting, but it certainly wasn't this blond giant with blazing pale blue eyes. A Viking in a tuxedo.

Zany spoke up. "Don't know where they came from, Sigurd. They just appeared out of nowhere."

The giant looked from Linny to Nicholas. Though he was wearing a tux, there was a savagery about him. He would definitely have been better suited to a cloak of wolf fur, with a bloody iron axe clutched in his fist.

Then he smiled and made it even worse. Was it possible to be frightened out of your wits and turned on at the same time?

"Did the Sorceress send you?" he said in a deep, gruff voice. "I smell that sneaky witch in all this."

Linny hadn't considered that. She turned to Nicholas. "Do you think she sent us here? You know her better than me."

Sigurd cast him a curious gaze. "You know the Sorceress? What is your name?" He made it sound like a command rather than a request.

Nicholas told him and Sigurd's smile dripped pure satisfaction. "Nicholas Darlington. I know you. You were supposed to join us here in the Dark World, but the witch changed her mind and kept you in the between-worlds." His smile turned evil. "I suppose she's changed it back again?"

Nicholas's jaw tightened.

"She hasn't changed her mind," Linny said, glaring at the Viking. "Nicholas lives in the mortal world now. Like I do."

"*You?* Mortal?" Sigurd's blue eyes gave Linny a leisurely and lustful sweep up and down.

"What did you think I was?" she mocked, her free hand on her hip. The other still clutched Nicholas's.

"One of the Sorceress's creatures? She has all kinds living in the between-worlds. Imps and fairies, dragons, hell hounds … she even has a water horse. Fair and beautiful, but deadly. I like women who bite."

They stared at each other. Sigurd's lips twitched and Nicholas cleared his throat, drawing their attention. "We both came here from the mortal world."

"And why would you do that?" Sigurd's raspy voice grew deeper, and suddenly he wasn't amused any more.

"Not through choice. We are hunting a damnable creature who calls himself Stewart," Nicholas answered. "The Sorceress has commanded us to capture him so that she can send him back to the underworld. He led us—"

"*Us?*"

"My friends and I, as well and Linny and her sister. Stewart lured us to a village in Scotland called Port Finlay. Then there was an explosion. And here we are."

"Stewart?" Sigurd repeated. His face was creased in a menacing frown. Beside him, Linny noticed Zany begin to edge away. "I know we are isolated here in the Dark World—the witch keeps us so—but I recognise that name. Stewart was here for a time. The Sorceress gave up on him, but still had hope. But I could tell he was irredeemable and in time she agreed. I sent him down to the underworld, where he belonged."

"Well he's not there now," Linny snapped.

Before Sigurd could answer, Nicholas went on. "There's more. Stewart is bringing demons into the mortal world, using them to weaken or distract us while we to try to recapture him. The latest one came from this realm, and Stewart told us that if we wanted to put a stop to its visits then we needed to find the source. That was just before the explosion."

"And here we are," Linny added, trying to replicate Nicholas's nonchalance.

Sigurd stared at them, and his blue eyes seemed to have grown brighter. Linny thought she could see movement in them, things swimming in a blue ocean. Her heart gave an unpleasant tug inside her chest, and she looked away. This was not good. She really needed to go home to Glasgow and pull the doona over her head.

"Stewart is in the underworld," the Lord of the Dark World insisted. "I sent him there myself and there is no escape from it. Does she think I set him upon the mortals for my own amusement? Is that what she thinks?" He glared at them furiously as if expecting a fight.

"I don't know what she thinks, but he found a way out and she has given us the task of handing him back to her." Nicholas spoke quietly, trying to de-escalate the situation. "If we fail, then one of us will end up taking his place in the underworld. That makes us quite motivated to do the job."

Sigurd wasn't really listening. Linny could see he was turning the facts over in his head, and then abruptly he turned those frightening eyes on the jester.

"*Zany!*" he roared, and the walls of the building shuddered in protest.

The little man didn't wait to hear what his master had to say. He sped off. Linny would never have believed a man with legs of different length could move so fast. Not that it made any difference. One moment he was bounding away furiously toward the door at the far end of the hall, and the next he was caught by an unseen force.

Struggling, shrieking, he was raised into the air and carried right back to them. He landed on the floor in front of Sigurd's shiny black wingtip shoes. The Dark Lord loomed over him in a way that promised very bad things in the jester's future.

"Tell me!" he roared. Now everything around them shook and rattled.

Zany huddled on the ground, trembling in terror, but Linny saw one of his eyes peek out from beneath his protectively folded arms. Instead of fear shining from it, there was a hint of sly cunning. When Sigurd knocked his arms away with his boot, Zany's expression morphed into one of repentance.

"He promised me," he whimpered. "He said he would be right back, that he just had an important message to deliver, and then he'd—"

"You mean you never sent him to the underworld!" More roaring from Sigurd. "You let him *out*?"

"He promised he'd come right back. He said—"

Sigurd stomped dangerously close to the little man's head, cracking the stone beneath. His eyes narrowed as he swooped down. "What did he promise you in return?" His voice suddenly became quiet and very dangerous.

For a moment it was as if Zany wasn't going to answer, then the words huffed out of him. "He said he'd arrange for me to spend an hour with Lady Leonore."

Sigurd blinked. "Well, I know you never spent that hour with her because you're still alive!" Sigurd stared at him a moment longer, his hands clenched at his sides, and then he strode across the hall to a steep set of stairs cut into the wall. "Interlopers! Both of you! Come with me!"

Linny looked at Nicholas. He appeared sombre, but when her eyes met his she could see something else. Concern. Nicholas Darlington was worried, and if he was worried then Linny had every reason to be petrified.

Chapter Seventeen

EVENTS WERE TAKING A DECIDED turn for the worse. Nicholas followed Linny to the stairs, trying not to notice the sway of her hips and the delicious shape of her form beneath her coat as she climbed. He'd become aware before that in moments of peril his physical urges increased to the point where he wanted nothing more than to lose himself in the arms—and between the legs— of a woman. Recently, that had meant *this* woman.

But he couldn't give in to those urges. Their survival depended on him keeping his wits about him, and the last thing he needed was to be distracted by his amorous impulses. Wasn't that what brought about his downfall in the first place?

Right now he wished he could talk to Lorne and Sutcliffe, and tell them what he had learnt. But the thought also made him edgy. Linny was worried about her sister, which made Nicholas wonder what would happen if his friends were gone. After all they had been through, the way their lives and even their fates had intertwined, being without them was something he found difficult to imagine.

He wanted to blame Stewart for the mess they were in. If Stewart had not escaped the Dark World and handed the Hellfire Club the means to summon the Destroyer, they could have gone on in blissful debaucherous ignorance. Nicholas would still be in 1808, living the life of a drunken womaniser … but also experiencing endless, soul destroying boredom.

He was shocked to hear that the Sorceress had nearly given up on him, that she had intended to send him on to the Dark World. Had she thought his crime too heinous, or that he was a man who could not be redeemed? Or both? Had she thought him to be a man like Stewart?

A dull pain throbbed in his chest. No. He was *nothing* like Stewart. He had proved himself to the Sorceress and to himself. He had changed from the man he had once been and had sworn he would never go back.

He locked his anger and pain out of the way. What was the point in imagining what might have happened had circumstances been different? It was more important to concentrate on the problem at hand. On the here and now.

At least there was one good thing about being in the Dark World. They knew Linny's demon had come from here. *Incubus.* If they could lure it to them and find a way out, they could lock it away behind them. There was no way he was going to let the foul creature touch her. The very thought made his blood boil. Nicholas would do everything in his power to deal with this problem before they left.

If they left.

Ahead of them, Sigurd moved through the murky shadows at the top of the staircase, toward another door. This one stood wide open and the room beyond was full of strange, shifting lights.

As they reached it Linny turned toward him. Her long blonde hair skimmed her shoulders, still tangled from the explosion, and her dark eyes were wide and full of questions. He tried to give her the reassurance she wanted with a smile, but he wasn't sure he was up to the task. How could he tell her what he was really thinking? Thus far he hadn't understood how they came to be here in The Dark World, except it had something to do with Stewart. And as Stewart's policy was divide and conquer then how were they to get home? Linny didn't belong here, but the incubus wanted her. What if it became necessary to bargain with Sigurd for her safe passage home, which might mean offering the Dark Lord something in return.

Nicholas Darlington.

So was he willing to give up his soul? Would he forsake the future he had hoped to find with Linny? He probably would, in fact he knew he would. Darlington had finally reached the tipping point the Sorceress was always going on about in that annoying manner, where he became a bloody hero.

"Nicholas," Linny whispered. They were just inside the room now, and his blood turned to ice as he followed her appalled gaze.

"This is the spinning room," their host said, his voice dripping with pleasure. Like the sadist he was, the bastard obviously enjoyed seeing the expressions on their faces. Nicholas tried to deny him that pleasure, but he wasn't sure he could hide his repugnance.

"Oh my God." Linny swallowed. "What…?"

He took another step forward, drawn to the scene despite himself. The room was full of the sound of movement, a low humming that made his teeth ache. There were cages suspended from the ceiling, and within those cages were people. Turning around and around. *Spinning.* He saw flashes of their torsos, arms, legs, and faces twisted in agony. The movement they made was jerky and unnatural, like the flickering strobe lights of a modern dance club that disrupted one's vision.

The people in those cages were captives, held by a dark twisting light that wrapped around them as they spun. This place was a prison, only worse, and these were the prisoners.

Linny clutched his arm. He felt her warm body pressed against his side. She was shaking. He wrapped his arm around her, pulling her close, and leaned into her. He could smell the sweet perfume of her skin, and the shampoo in her hair. It was comforting, but it was also wrong.

She shouldn't be here. She shouldn't be seeing any of this. Someone like her had done nothing to deserve being anywhere near this place. She had been taken out of her ordinary, normal life and thrown her into a world she couldn't understand, one that was going to leave her broken and torn and perhaps even kill her.

"Lady Leonore!" Sigurd had taken up position in front of one of the cages. Nicholas thought he saw a woman's face tip down, dark hair flying, eyes as black as the grave. There was a sound like laughter, and then she turned her back on them and he caught a glimpse of white buttocks as she lifted her skirts.

Sigurd muttered a curse, but at the same time he was smirking. It seemed that the lady was a thorn in his side, but perhaps not one he intended to remove anytime soon.

"How many … these poor people … how many of them are here?" Linny was attempting to process what was in front of her. Trying to make sense of the impossible. Nicholas had often felt the same way when he was in the between-worlds.

"Ten prisoners, in this room," Sigurd said, his massive arms crossed. "Sometimes there's more."

"How long do you keep them?" she asked.

"As long as is necessary for them to come to an acceptance of their crimes," he said dismissively. "None of these souls deserve your pity, pretty mortal. I assure you, there is a reason they are here, and their punishment is just."

Sigurd's gaze moved to Nicholas. The look Sigurd gave wasn't one he felt comfortable with, and considering what the Dark Lord had revealed to him a short while ago, he felt as if Sigurd was measuring him up for a cage of his own. It was time to change the subject.

"The demon that Stewart has sent to plague Linny," he said. "I want to track it down and stop it."

That smirk again, as if Sigurd found such noble intentions amusing, or perhaps he just didn't believe it. Being the Dark Lord no doubt came with a high degree of scepticism when assessing the motives of others.

"Can we do that?" Linny asked. Her dark eyes shone with hope. She turned from Sigurd to Nicholas and back again. "Can we stop it?"

Sigurd didn't look convinced, or perhaps that was his natural expression. Darlington admitted he had taken a dislike to the big man, and not just because the Dark Lord had hinted that he belonged locked up in one of those spinning cages. It was the way he looked at Linny. She was a beautiful woman and one he had begun to consider belonged to him. Even if the feeling could not be said to be mutual.

"Tell me about this demon that is plaguing you, pretty girl," Sigurd began in a deep rumble. "I need to know more if I am going to put a stop to Stewart's games."

"I've only really seen it in dreams. Not in the flesh. But Nicholas has. He stayed awake so that I could sleep." She shot a sideways glance to Nicholas. He could see her fear and how she bravely tried not to show it.

"It only appears when Linny sleeps," Nicholas continued, and proceeded to describe the thing. "I don't know what its intentions are but I assume..."

He met Linny's eyes again. "We believe it is an incubus."

Sigurd snorted. "And not a very attractive one by the sound of it."

Linny rolled her eyes. "Why do men think women only have to see a handsome man and she'll roll over on her back for him?"

Sigurd gave her another of those interested glances, and Nicholas quickly drew their attention back to the demon.

"As I explained before, it was Stewart who said that the incubus comes from the Dark World. He also said that to stop its visits to the mortal world we needed to track it down in its lair."

"He's right in that, at least. If a portal has been opened then we must close it." Once again he ran his eyes over Linny. Nicholas had to clench his teeth and stop himself from pulling her safely behind him. Sigurd must have been aware of the affect he was having because he gave Nicholas a satisfied smirk. The next moment he shouted "Zany!" and made them jump.

The little man appeared as suddenly as he had disappeared, standing before his master with his head thrown back, looking way up. His expression was one of subservience and complete contrition, but Nicholas did not believe that for a moment. Zany was keen on deception.

"This is all your doing," Sigurd reminded the jester. "Fix it, or by the hammer of Thor I will have you spinning by the morning!"

Zany blanched. "Yes, my lord."

Sigurd leaned closer, crowding the little man as if to deprive him of oxygen. "And I haven't decided how to punish you for the rest of it. You released a dangerous madman onto an unsuspecting mortal world for an hour with *that* woman? Your penance is something the Sorceress and I will have to discuss. Together."

Zany flinched. Sigurd gave him one last look and then straightened his tux and walked away. Soon they were alone with the jester, and the awful sights and sounds of the spinning cages.

Zany risked a look at Lady Leonore, who was facing them again. Nicholas heard her soft laughter, or maybe he was just imagining it. The humming gave him a headache and he wondered bleakly what it must be like to be held in this place. What had these prisoners done to be considered suitable fodder for the Dark World? Closer to eternal damnation than even he himself had been?

"Nicholas?" Linny whispered. He saw a flash of sympathy in her face, before it returned to a ferocious frown. "Can we do what we have to do and then get out of this place?" she demanded. "I need to find Maggie."

"We'll find her," he said, but they both knew his comforting words were without substance. They were both left to the whims of this world and those within it.

Linny turned her furious attention to Zany. "Did you really let that creep Stewart into our world?" she hissed. "Do you have any idea how many people he's killed? If he's hurt my sister I will come back here and help your master put you in one of these things." She waved her hand toward the cages. "Do you hear me?"

Zany bobbed his head. "Yes, my lady."

Nicholas wondered why the little man continued to roam free in this place when he was so obviously untrustworthy. Maybe it was difficult to find servants in the Dark World, so Sigurd put up with him. Or perhaps his usefulness outweighed his treachery. All the same, Nicholas wasn't sure he would dismiss the big man's threats as easily as Zany seemed inclined to. Sigurd and the Sorceress—now that was a formidable pair.

Again he felt Linny's warm body against his, pressing into him for comfort and reassurance. The thought that she looked to him for such things brought an ache to his chest and a ridiculous urge to smile.

Then he remembered what had happened to the last woman who'd been under his so-called care. He should tell her about his past. He should have done so already. But right now she needed to trust him and he wasn't sure she would, not if she knew the truth about Nicholas Darlington.

He turned to the jester. "Show us how to close the portal," he demanded. "Our friends in the mortal world need us. We have to get home."

Zany looked genuinely surprised. "The first I can do, but the second? Whether or not you ever leave this place is not up to me, but the Dark Lord."

Linny groaned and put her face in her hands. "Don't tell me that," she muttered to herself. "You can't tell me that anything I've done remotely warrants me spending eternity here. A few unpaid parking tickets, that's all!"

"But you *are* here, and since only people who deserve to be here are here, you must deserve it."

"But the Sorceress didn't send me here, pal. Isn't she supposed to be the only one who can do that?"

"She is, and since you are here, she must have sent you. It's all very logical, you see."

"I can't believe I might be condemned to eternal torment on a technicality!"

"First things first," Nicholas interrupted before she could lose it completely. "Explain to us how we stop the demon, Zany. The Sorceress believes there is something tethering it to Linny, an invisible thread that needs to be cut. How do we do that?"

The little man nodded his head, striking a thoughtful pose. "You will first need to draw him out," he said. "Pretty lady has to fall asleep. Then, when he comes, you have to snare him and hold him. Only then can we cut whatever magic it is that holds them together. After that we must close the portal so that he doesn't escape again."

It sounded simple. Too simple. Nicholas eyed him suspiciously, but Linny couldn't contain her joy. "Then let's do it!" she shouted.

Zany pumped a fist, bounded up and down, and then took off out of the spinning room. Nicholas paused and, unable to help himself, took a last glance over his shoulder at the souls trapped in their cages. That could have been him. It still might be.

Linny's hand closed on his. "You don't really think Sigurd would keep you here?" she asked him anxiously, her eyes searching his so that he wondered what she saw in them. "Why would the Sorceress let him do that? You're changed. Whatever you did before, you're a better man now. Your life is with us."

She looked away, realising what she had said. He wasn't sure whether she was embarrassed or worried he might think she had made a declaration when she had not intended to do so. Maybe she just didn't want to seem vulnerable. She worked hard to keep her softer side hidden. To throw aside her usual caution to comfort him now meant a great deal to him.

From the first time he had seen her in Maggie's cottage, there had been a connection between them. He knew she had felt it too. He'd missed her when they were apart, him in the between-worlds and she in Glasgow. And once they had been brought back together again, those feelings he had for her only intensified. He was beginning to want things he had never wanted before. Want a life he had never believed possible before.

"Let's deal with your demon first," he said. His face was so close to hers he could feel her breath. "After that, we'll worry about getting out of here." Her scent filled his head, blocking out the lingering hint of sulphur in the air, and he was tempted to simply stand there and soak her in.

Linny nodded in uncharacteristic compliance.

"Maggie is all right," he added in a confident tone. "Lorne wouldn't have it any other way."

Her smile was genuine, but he could see doubt circling in her eyes. Eyes bright with unshed tears. Linny's tough exterior was beginning to crack and Nicholas was determined to help put her back together should she fall apart.

Chapter Eighteen

LINNY WONDERED WHETHER SHE SHOULD be worried. They were in a corridor that seemed to go on for miles. Once Zany had led them back down into the great hall, they went through more doors and ante rooms, and then down more stairs until they reached this corridor. The one that seemed to go on forever. First the walls were covered with wood panelling, then bare stone blocks. The air felt heavy and full of foreboding.

Nicholas was holding her hand, so she concentrated on the reassuring strength in his fingers and his wide palm. They'd been holding hands a lot recently. It wasn't something she could remember doing with other men. Keith had had a thing about too much touching in public—except when he was drunk and then she couldn't keep him off her—and none of the others had stayed around long enough for her to want to show them any affection.

This was different. *He* was different.

And Linny felt different when she was with him, too. It was as if he could see all of her, even the difficult and complicated bits. And unlike other men he still wanted her, and was willing to do whatever he could to please her. It calmed her anxieties. And then there was the sneaky pleasure of wondering how it would feel to kiss him again, to touch him and to take him to bed. She already knew it would feel amazing, but that didn't mean she wasn't scared to take the final step.

Another woman might just toss aside her doubts and go for the ride. But although Linny might act like the sort of person who was willing to take such a risk, that wasn't who she really was. She had been hurt too many times, and when you were afraid of being hurt again you have trouble letting anyone in too deep.

And yet, somehow, Nicholas had slipped past her guard and now he was inside her head, and before too long he'd be inside her body too. And her heart? Once he was in there, there would be no getting him out.

Falling in love with Nicholas Darlington had never been on Linny's agenda. Quite the opposite. She wasn't sure what she was going to do about it.

Somewhere up ahead there was a rattle of stone. She froze. There was a picture in her head, a combination of fear and darkness and her stumbling on and on, looking for a way out. She pushed it away.

"What is it?" Nicholas's asked, his breath against her ear so warm it brought out goosebumps. She wanted to press her lips to his and lose herself in sensation, a sense of something real and tangible here to hold onto. Instead she forced a scowl onto her face.

"I have a nasty sense of déjà vu."

"From when you were here before?" They were walking again and up ahead was another door.

"Well I must have been here, right? If my little friend followed me back somehow. I get these flashbacks. Nothing solid, but this does feel familiar. It just doesn't seem as frightening as I thought it would. Maybe because you're here…"

He looked surprised at first. Then his eyebrow quirked up and he smiled.

Oh, well done, Linny! Way to keep him at a distance!

But there wasn't time for him to say anything, or for her to backpedal. Because they were now at their destination, inside whatever room Zany had been leading them to. Nicholas muttered a good old English curse under his breath and they drew to a halt. His hand tightened on hers.

Reluctantly, Linny followed his gaze. The room was just a room, with the walls on either side and behind them set in the now familiar grey stone, but right in front of them where there should have been a fourth wall, there was only darkness.

She frowned, wondering if it was just the usual lack of reflective light that made her think that if she took a few more steps forward she would fall into a void. It felt like some space movie, where the main character was about to be sucked into an abyss.

The hairs rose on the back of her neck as the smell of sulphur in the air grew stronger. Zany watched them with sly amusement, evidently pleased with their response. "Your demon's in there," he said. "Somewhere."

"What? I'm not going in there!" She heard her voice quaver.

"No, I would not advise it," Zany pulled a sympathetic face. "That is the entrance to the underworld."

"You said—"

"Yes, I said the demon came from here. As well as being the entry to the underworld, there are caves in there. A whole catacomb of them. It is where Sigurd keeps his pets. The Sorceress has her private zoo, and so does he. Believe me, pretty lady, *anyone* who values their sanity would not go past this point."

"Then how are we supposed to get hold of the incubus?" she asked, trying not to stare too long into the abyss. She was afraid it might start staring back. She was not sure even Nicholas could stop her from running if that happened.

She glanced at him and saw that he was still staring. As if he was fascinated by the inky darkness, and she worried that, like someone afraid of heights who had the strange urge to jump, he was going to take a running leap into it. She tightened her grip on his hand, just in case.

"The incubus comes to you when you sleep, yes?" Zany said, waiting for her nod. "Then you must sleep, while the earl keeps watch, and when the incubus approaches, he will snare it. Done." Zany smirked and clapped his hands.

"Sleep?" She looked about her at the grubby floor. "Here?"

Zany chuckled as if he found her tone amusing. "No, pretty mortal, not here. The demon will need to be returned to this place once the tether is broken and the portal it is using is closed. But you ... come, follow me. I have had a room prepared for you."

She was relieved to turn her back on that creepy void and they followed him back down the corridor, but not too far. Linny noticed a door set in the wall and Zany reached up and turned an iron ring with both hands. The thick wooden panels creaked open like something out of a horror movie, which seemed entirely appropriate.

Things were very different inside, and she caught her breath in surprise. It was like something straight out of a period drama. A fire burned in a carved stone fireplace opposite the door, but in between was an antique four poster bed. Apart from the draperies, which were a dark blue, it reminded her of the bed in Maggie's penthouse. Luscious and tempting. Seductive.

The sort of bed you could spend time in with the man of your dreams.

Despite the muddle of thoughts in her head and the fear in her heart, Linny felt an ache of desire. Nicholas seemed fascinated by the bed as well.

Great. How was she supposed to steel her heart when all she wanted to do was lose herself in the arms of this Regency rake?

Linny noticed a side table, on which a tray of food and a decanter of what looked like red wine was set out. Who had done all of this? She looked about suspiciously, wondering where the invisible servants were hiding. Or had it been whipped up by magic? Perhaps Sigurd had just waved his arms and everything was done.

"So you want me to go to sleep here and just wait?"

Without answering, Zany bounced over to a trunk against the wall and threw it open—there was a clunk as the lid hit the panelling. He dragged out something that looked like a fishermen's net. Bundling it up into his arms, he brought it over to them. Linny stared at it doubtfully.

"You are thinking the incubus can claw his way out of this," Zany he said and smiled. Suddenly, he threw the net up into the air. As it came down lights came on all over it, sparkling and winking like a horde of fireflies. The moment it hit the floor the lights snuffed out again.

Pleased with their reaction, Zany said, "When the demon is close enough, throw this over him. He won't be able to escape, and once he is captured, call for me and I will secure him, cut the tether and return him to the void."

Nicholas looked at the net. "Won't he put up a fight?"

"Probably, but once he is caught he can't escape and he can't harm anyone. Remember, your pretty mortal is counting on you. You must wait for your moment and strike at the right time, my Earl of Northcote."

Nicholas probably hadn't liked being called that. He glanced at her, and tried to give a reassuring smile.

"There is food and wine if you need more time," Zany went on, pointing at the tray, "but do not drink too much and miss your opportunity. I do not know if Sigurd will allow you another one."

"Oh, so no pressure then," Linny mumbled. "What a relief."

Nicholas leaned into her and she stared into his tea coloured eyes, so warm and comforting.

"It will be all right," he said quietly. "Trust me, Linny."

She found herself nodding, because she did. She did trust him. Surprisingly, she trusted this man when she had never trusted a man before. She trusted him with her life.

Zany cleared his throat and she heard a hint of laughter in the sound. "Sweet dreams then," he said, then cocked one of his outrageous shoes and gave a low bow, before he bounced to the door and closed it firmly behind him.

Linny looked at the door, wondering for a moment if she would ever see the other side of it. Then she wondered if she would ever see her sister again. She took a deep breath. Time to focus. She needed to relax enough to sleep, so that the demon would come creeping in, and then Nicholas could throw that firefly net over it.

How on earth was she going to do *that*?

Nicholas limped over to the tray and stood a moment, inspecting it. He looked over his shoulder, his dark hair loose about his face, his scar invisible from this angle. "You should eat. Perhaps have a glass of wine."

She came to join him. "How about two?" The tray was laden with succulent treats and her mouth actually watered. It felt as if it had been an eternity since she had last eaten. Maybe time moved differently here in the Dark World? What if a hundred years had gone by in the blink of an eye? What if she arrived home in Glasgow and everyone she knew was dead and dust? What if it was the other way around, and she arrived back before anyone noticed she was gone? Her head started to hurt.

Nicholas's warm palm cupped her face. "You're thinking too much," he said. "You need to *not* think. Just relax."

"Easy for you to say. You're not the one who summons a horny demon toad by falling asleep."

Nicholas smirked. "Come."

He held out his hand and didn't intend to take no for an answer. She barely hesitated, having already made up her mind to put her trust in him. He smiled down at her as she took his hand, as if he was fully aware of her inner struggles, before leading her to the bed.

It was so high up that she wondered how she would get onto it, but a moment later Nicholas's hands closed around her waist and the next thing she knew she was sitting on the edge of the mattress, her boots dangling far above the floor below.

He knelt to remove them for her.

She wanted to tell him that she could undress herself, but there was something humbling in the way he gently slid the boots from her feet, and set them aside. He was treating her like a precious thing, and she had never been treated like that before, not by anyone. She didn't know whether to laugh or burst into tears.

When he was finished he gave a sly smile, and she knew he had enjoyed ministering to her but didn't want to tell her so. He moved back to the food tray and soon returned with a full plate.

"Thank you," she said quietly, taking a grape. It was almost black and so juicy. She had expected a realm like this to cater more to the gnawing the meat on the bone variety of customer. This felt almost classy and she breathed a sigh of contentment as she bit into the succulent fruit. It tasted as good as it looked. "Try one," she said, looking up at him.

He watched her mouth in a way that made everything inside her go tight. Needy. Nicholas was different to all the other men she'd known, and it had been so long since she been with one. Part of her desperately needed the release. Right now. But she didn't want just any man. She wanted *him*.

She watched him walk back to the table to get his own plate and then he joined her on the bed, leaving a foot of space between them. Was he being thoughtful? He must be aware of how intimate this moment was between them, so perhaps he was just being cautious. Or perhaps he didn't want to distract her from the task at hand.

"Let's get comfortable," she said, and shuffled her way to the headboard, pushing the pillows up so that she had something to lean on. She crossed her ankles and began to eat. He soon followed, sitting at her side but still at a respectable distance.

There was a long silence but eventually she had to return to the question that had been jumping around in her head since she'd woken up.

"Do you think they're alive?" Her voice wobbled, and Nicholas gave her a concerned look. The secret she had been holding in up till now burst out of her. "Maggie is pregnant."

Nicholas froze. Even in her anguish she felt the change in him, from comforting to horrified. His face went white and his eyes brimmed with suffering. There was more to this than the pain he was feeling for the possible loss of his friends.

"With child," he said through colourless lips. He pushed his tray of food aside and ran a hand down his face, stopping at the scar and fingering it so roughly she wondered whether the flesh would tear open.

"I didn't think it was a good idea either," she said. "I mean, as much as we're all hoping the Sorceress won't be a complete dick about things, it's just as likely Lorne'll have to go back to the past. Maggie will be left alone with the baby."

Nicholas shook his head. "I understand why they wanted a child together. Once he's gone, then at least she has something remaining of him. And wherever he is, he will know a part of him is still with her. They probably find comfort in that."

"That's what Maggie said."

They sat in silence on the bed for a moment, so close and yet miles apart.

"I hope she's alive. Her and the baby. And Lorne. And Aiden. And Loki. I mean, really, I hope nobody else got hurt."

Nicholas smirked. "As do I." He reached out an arm and pulled her to his side. Now the silence was comforting, until she started to think about the black void in the other room, and wonder when her own personal demon was going to appear in the corner of the room and begin its crawl toward her. A shiver ran over her skin and she clutched Nicholas a little tighter.

"I never want children," she said, her voice muffled. "There's too much to worry about when you bring another human being into the world. I had enough trouble looking after Maggie, and she wasn't a baby. I don't think I could cope with something that small and helpless."

She could hear him breathing. Had what she had said upset him? Perhaps he had children of his own? Really she knew so little about him. He had not spoken of his past, not in detail. She knew he had secrets. When Sigurd had told them Nicholas had once been destined for the spinning room, she couldn't help but speculate as to why. If the punishment was meant to fit the crime, then what had he done that was so truly awful? He had told her on the way to Port Finlay that he had taken a life through negligence. There was no way she could misinterpret that, but she needed detail. Context. Sigurd had said that the prisoners in that room had to admit to their crimes, to own them, and surely Nicholas had admitted to his, or the Sorceress wouldn't have set him free?

Yet this man wasn't a criminal. There was nothing evil about him, not like Stewart. He was Nicholas, and she trusted him as well as liked him. Well, to be honest, she more than liked him. Her body craved him, and right now she was on the verge of giving in to those cravings.

His lips brushed against her hair. "You need to sleep," he said.

"I can't," she replied. "I'm too tense."

Come on, ask me what you can do to make me less tense.

His fingers stroked her shoulder and upper arm. Her head was nestled against his chest and if she lifted it a little she could taste his bare skin with her tongue. *Why not?* The temptation was so strong she had to fight it with every ounce of her will power.

"What can I do to help you feel … less tense?"

Had he really said that? When she didn't answer he leaned his head back to see her face. She burrowed deeper into his chest, but he lifted her chin and forced her to meet his gaze.

"Linny?"

She couldn't hide it. She didn't try. He must be able to see every longing, every desire, written right there on her face. He must be able to hear it on her every breath, even smell her desire for him on her.

His expression changed. The bones of his face seemed sharper, while his eyes were darker. He stroked his thumb over her lips, back and forth.

"Are you sure?" he asked her, but he was already leaning forward to kiss her. When she didn't answer he stopped. Just … stopped.

She couldn't stand it any longer. "Please," she moaned, and launched herself into his arms.

Chapter Nineteen

———◆———

SHE TASTED AS GOOD AS he'd remembered. That was his first thought. His second was wondering how the hell was he going to stop himself from eating her alive.

He hadn't had a woman in two hundred years, and he wanted her. He was desperate for her. Ravenous. Here they were in the Dark World, hoping to capture a demon, with a chance that he would never leave, and all he could think of was getting inside this woman.

He lifted his head and took a breath, ready to tell her that this was a mistake.

She put her fingers over his lips, and as her eyes searched his, dark and shining and a little wild, he realised she had read his thoughts perfectly. "No second guessing," she said in her bossy voice. "We both need this. Just go with it, Nicholas. Even if it's only once."

He didn't argue. Instead he kissed her fingers, taking them into his mouth. Her eyes widened, surprised, and that made him smile. He took her hand in his, kissing her palm. "I'm in complete agreement," he said, although that wasn't entirely true. He'd just gone past the point of no return.

She blinked, slightly dazed, watching his mouth. "Good."

He tried not to groan as he leaned in and took her mouth with his. Her lips were soft and warm, and the tip of her tongue brushed against his. He cupped her cheeks and slanted her face so that he could dive deeper.

Her breasts were pressed against his chest, and the points of her nipples were evident through her top. She'd taken off her coat and sweater, and the blouse underneath was made of some silky material. He reached to cup one firm mound, his thumb rubbing back and forwards over its peak. She arched against him, and he nuzzled against her throat, licking its hollow, and felt her thigh against his hip. She lifted her leg over his lap, tensing it around him as she clung to him even tighter.

If he wasn't careful this was going to be over far too soon, and he wanted it to last. He wanted more than just once. He wanted to keep her and he wasn't sure how he could. Now he understood how Lorne felt about Maggie—that heart skittering sense of need and longing, while at the same time knowing it could all go terribly wrong.

She had lifted herself so that her legs were curled up either side of his hips, and he could feel the heat of her against his cock. He was so hard he hurt, and he felt a mixture of ecstasy and agony when she ground against him, making little sounds in her throat, her mouth on his. It was the most erotic thing he had ever heard and he rolled her over and pressed down, letting her feel him, all of him.

"Nicholas." Her head fell back, her fair hair spread out on the pillows. He ran his lips down her throat, unbuttoning her blouse as he went, little kisses and then his tongue over the swell of her breasts above the lacy black cups of her bra. Underwear in this modern age was so much better. None of those endless buttons and laces, never mind all the fumbling to find what he wanted. No wonder he had simply tossed a woman's skirts up over her head and rutted like an animal before. Then again, that probably hadn't been the fault of the underwear. That had been the fault of the man.

Linny's fingers tangled in his hair, her fingernails scratched against his scalp in a way that made him even harder. He reached up and nipped her plump bottom lip, then soothed it with his tongue, before kissing her again. He already dreamed about her mouth but the reality was so much better.

She fumbled with her jeans, trying to undo the button and zip them undone at the same time. A moment later he'd helped strip her bare. He'd hesitated over her panties, they were black too and so thin and delicate he wanted to look at them more closely.

Perhaps next time.

His hand slid between her thighs, finding her so wet he groaned aloud. She wanted him. It was enough to make him come in his breeches. Except that she was tugging them down, her fingers digging into his thighs, and then his buttocks as she pulled him back to where she wanted him.

"Please…" she panted. "I want you."

He could wait no longer. He pushed the tip against her folds, feeling her wet heat. She pushed back against him, and he felt himself slide into heaven.

After Italy, he had always covered up before laying with a woman. It wasn't the same, the lambskin condoms were unpleasant, but necessary. For the first time since then he was bare and for a moment he hesitated, unsure of how to proceed.

"Don't need a condom. I'm on the pill," she said impatiently, and he understood that answered his unasked question.

The next moment he was deep inside. She was running her hands over his body, her mouth was on his, and he wasn't going to stop. He was never going to stop.

"Nicholas," she whispered. "Harder."

He complied, pushing her up against the pillows.

"*Harder,*" she repeated.

The sound of their flesh slapping together, the tight sensation of him inside her and her muscles squeezing him, his mouth hot on her throat and the noises she was making. It was exquisite, it was bliss. He wasn't going to last much longer.

"Linny," he moaned.

"I'm nearly…" she breathed. Suddenly her body clenched around his, milking him, so that he had no option but to go with her.

Their voices mingled, unintelligible, pleasure in

every sound. Then the collapse.

They lay together, his body pressing her down into the mattress, chests heaving, sated.

It took a while for him to regain his senses. As he lay there he could feel her run her fingers across his unshaven jaw, her breathing returning to normal. He didn't want to move, so he pressed closer, closing his eyes, enjoying her soft touch. It wouldn't take much for him to slip away into slumber. Then he remembered he had to stay awake, and why. He tensed and forced his eyes open.

"Linny?"

"Hmmm?"

"Go to sleep now. Can you?"

Her mouth twitched up at the corners. "Hmm-hmm."

He chuckled and leaned in to kiss her lips, once for each corner, and then another deeper one. He wanted her again but this wasn't the time. He levered himself up. "Goodnight," he whispered.

"Night." A moment later she was asleep.

He could have watched her for the rest of the night—well, he assumed it was night, the Dark World didn't have any time keeping devices on display—but he had work to do. Nicholas climbed off the bed, straightened his clothing and ran a hand back through his hair. His body was lighter, the burdens he'd been carrying seemed to have been lifted off him, and he found himself smiling for no reason.

He looked back at the woman on the bed, her fair hair bright even in the shadows, her hand tucked under her cheek. She looked small on the large expanse of the bed, and her naked skin glowed like alabaster. He pulled up the covers and spread them over her, tucking her in, pausing to sweep the pad of his thumb along her flushed cheek.

Pretty girl, Sigurd had called her. Pretty mortal. But she was more than that. She was brave and strong, and behind that bristling exterior she showed to the world to protect herself, was a woman who was all heart. By claiming her body, his feelings for her had only deepened. He wanted her more than ever now, and he was going to make sure that the incubus that had been making her life a misery never bothered her again.

His own future looked less than certain right now, but at least he could protect Linny, and he would, come what may.

Chapter Twenty

NICHOLAS COULDN'T SAY HOW MANY hours had passed—they seemed to tick over so very slowly. Once again he bemoaned the fact that there was no means of tracking time in this world. At first he'd lounged in the chair by the table, popping grapes and sliced figs and crumbly bits of cheese into his mouth, followed by sips of red wine. His mind was full of Linny's soft body and the pleasure they'd found in each other. His chest felt tight as he remembered being buried deep inside her, and the little sounds she'd made against the hollow of his throat. He wanted to do it again, but this matter had to take precedence. She needed to sleep.

He glanced over at the bed, listening to her soft breathing and the crackle of the flames as the fire died down. It was getting colder. He remembered how the temperature in Linny's bedroom had seemed to drop when he had kept watch over her. Right before the demon appeared.

He peered into the gloom of the corners, looking all around in case the monster tried to creep up behind him. Nothing. After a time he began to wonder if the incubus would come at all. Perhaps she needed to be in the mortal world to draw its attention. Perhaps it was in Linny's house right now, waiting for her. Maybe Zany was wrong about the incubus. Maybe the jester was just telling them what they wanted to hear.

It had been a long day. His belly was full and he had made love to the woman he desired above all others. The only woman he'd ever desired beyond carnal pleasures. Nicholas felt wonderfully relaxed and despite all his efforts to keep them open, his eyes began to close.

He didn't know how long he was asleep. He was dreaming about spinning in one of those cages, the force of its movement making his eyes bulge and his head pound. There was a flash of Lenore's face, beautiful and yet ghoulish, taunting him from the edge of his sight. That was enough to bring him back and the next moment he was awake. Awareness returned immediately. There was an icy sensation in the room. It was so cold that when he breathed a white cloud formed.

In that moment between nightmare and reality, he struggled to make sense of what he saw before him. The creature was on Linny's bed, only inches away from her sleeping form. It was within seconds of putting its filthy paws on the woman he loved.

Nicholas's heart was pounding. He wanted to lurch up out of his chair and throw himself at it, but he stopped himself. That wouldn't work. The demon would simply go back to its bolthole and the opportunity to capture it would be lost.

He took a deep, slow breath. He had a job to do. Slowly, he reached down to the side of his chair and closed his hand on the net.

Maybe the demon heard him. He wasn't sure. Regardless, it turned its head and let out a half snarl and half hiss, showing sharp teeth. It leapt toward Linny at the same time as Darlington hurled the net over it.

Lights flashed, the colours blinding in the dim room. When he could see again, the demon was tangled in the net, in a violent struggle on the bed, trying to escape. Linny woke up and screamed, pushing herself toward the headboard, her eyes terrified as she saw the writhing ball of fury.

Darlington ran to the other side of the bed to drag her up into his arms, holding her close as he backed them out of reach. The demon flailed, its glowing eyes malevolent.

"Thank you," Linny breathed into the crook of his neck. "Thank you, Nicholas. Thank you. Thank—"

"Hush." He was shaking as well. He didn't tell her that he had almost messed the whole thing up. What mattered was that he had done it. He pushed the alternative endings out of his mind, clinging to the positives.

The door creaked as it opened and Zany bounced in. His face was lit with glee as he spotted the snared demon. The creature, seeing him, seemed to know its days of liberty were over and suddenly quietened, giving one last vengeful hiss. Nicholas stepped in front of Linny to give her some privacy as she began hastily to dress.

"Ah-ha!" the jester said, and rubbed his hands together. "I am impressed." He gave Nicholas a sly look, making him wonder just how much the little man had seen. Perhaps he had a spy hole somewhere in the room. And that meant he had watched them… The thought added a wave of anger to all the other emotions he was dealing with.

"Sigurd has gone to visit the between-worlds," Zany said. "It seems that a large number of mortals are cluttering up the Sorceress's domain, all of them very confused. They have arrived from that place you spoke of. Port Finlay."

Linny jerked up her head as she finished buttoning up her coat. "Port Finlay?" she squeaked. "Is my sister one of them?"

Zany shrugged, but there was a wariness about him. "I don't know the details. The witchy woman isn't very happy. No she isn't. She's asked Sigurd to explain himself, as if my lord was somehow responsible. Once he gets there I'm sure he'll soon decide it was *my* fault." He appeared downcast but Nicholas knew by now that this was all an act. Zany didn't have an honest bone in his twisted body.

"You know he means to keep you here in the Dark World?" he said to Nicholas, biting his lip. "You do understand that, don't you? You're his bargaining chip when it comes to the Sorceress."

Linny looked from one to the other, and what she saw made her even more agitated. "No," she said, shaking her head. "He can't do that! Can he?"

Nicholas wanted to give her some hope, but he feared that Zany was right. "Linny—"

"I won't let him," she said stubbornly.

"He can't keep either of us," Nicholas found the words. "The Sorceress wouldn't allow it."

Zany gave him a look. "You know that's not true, my Earl of Northcote. If Sigurd wants to keep you so that he can play games with the witch, then there is nothing you can do about it. I know him well. He is going to offer to let the pretty lady go, because he knows you'll play the hero. Your life for hers. But I think you already knew that."

Nicholas glared at Zany, but it wasn't the jester he was angry with. He was angry because it seemed that, no matter what he did or how hard he strived, his fate remained in the hands of others.

Linny's fingers tangled with his. She was his right now and he wanted to savour this moment. His fate might not be his to decide, but he was determined that he would do all in his power to save Linny. He would sacrifice himself to save his woman, and do so gladly.

"The Sorceress won't let you keep Nicholas," she was still arguing the point with Zany. "She wants him to succeed."

The little man shrugged. "But it isn't the Sorceress who rules here. Sigurd controls the Dark World and he clings to his little kingdom because it is all he has. If he sees benefit in keeping him here, to keep a leash on the witch, then he will. They have a history together that goes back centuries. They are playing a game, one they both want to win. Ultimately it doesn't matter what happens to you, my dear Earl of Northcote."

Linny's breath turned shaky. Nicholas wondered if she was going to cry and he couldn't bear that. "You can't keep him," she whispered. "It isn't fair."

His longing for her and a life with her almost undid him. "Linny? My love?"

She shook her head, refusing to look at him, so he grasped her chin gently so that she had no choice.

"Linny, I will do what needs to be done," he said in a resolute voice. He would be the man the Sorceress always said he could be, and yet it felt like a hollow victory. Because Nicholas was sentencing himself to a life here among the outcasts and the murderers. After all his work to be a better man he was going to still end up punished, and yet if it meant saving Linny then he couldn't regret his sacrifice.

Linny refused to give in. "No. I won't… Nicholas, I can't let you do this…"

"Perhaps this is why I was brought here," Nicholas said. "To *save* you. To give my life for yours. I can accept that."

"Well I can't!"

And then Zany said quietly, "Perhaps there is another way."

Chapter Twenty-One

LINNY HAD HOPED THAT IF she kept telling Nicholas she wasn't going to let him do
this, that she could save him. If she continued to
argue with him, he might eventually stop respond-
ing in that horribly reasonable voice and let her
win. Because everything around her felt shaky and
uncertain and she was very much afraid she was
going to lose. That she would leave the Dark World
without him. How was that fair? He had snared the
demon, he'd proved himself in every possible way,
and now he was going to be left behind as a pawn
between two supernatural arseholes? She wouldn't
allow it, she told herself, terrified and angry at the
same time. She just wouldn't!

There is another way.

Zany's interruption had brought an end to their
stalemate. "What other way?" she asked. The jester
was a slippery character, she had already learned
that, and she didn't trust him, not one bit, but right
now he was all they had.

"I can send you back to the mortal world,

through the same portal the incubus was using. Before I close it."

A surge of hope. She tried not to let it over-whelm her.

Nicholas frowned, although she had seen the spark of hope in his eyes too. "Why would you do that? And how do we know you'll do as you say?"

Zany put his arms over his head and groaned in frustration. "Simple self-preservation, my Earl of Northcote. Because Sigurd is going to tell the Sorceress about Stewart. She'll know it was me and she'll want to punish me. If I help you, my Earl of Northcote, then you can *tell* her I helped you. You can get me on the witch's good side."

"Her good side?" Linny snorted because other-wise she might cry. "Does she have one?"

Zany dropped his arms and gave Nicholas a melting look that was clearly meant to win him over. "She *likes* you. She won't want you down here after all that she's done to save you. If I return you to the mortal world she'll be more inclined to forgive me. Every little bit helps."

"What about Sigurd? He won't be happy you let me go."

Zany gave a grimace. "As I said, the Sea Strider and the Sorceress have a past. Whatever I do now will rile him, and I cannot please them both, so I must choose a side. Preferably the one that results in the least pain. I choose the witch."

He had it all worked out. Linny nudged Nicholas with her shoulder. She could see he was tired—well of course he was, he hadn't slept—but there was also a gleam in his brown eyes that hadn't been there a moment ago.

"What do you think?" she asked him.

"Sounds plausible," his voice was raspy. "Though it's a risk."

Zany huffed. "*I'm* the one taking the risk. In trying to please the witchy woman I'm going to make Sigurd angry. *Angrier*."

"Are you telling me that you live in this awful place with that giant and yet you are more frightened of the witchy woman?" she said.

Zany nodded rapidly. "Aren't you?"

Linny turned to Nicholas and rolled her eyes. He grinned and took her hand in his, lifting it to his lips. She felt herself melt. "All right," he said to Zany, "We shall do this. And if it all works out then we will consider your request."

Zany looked as if that wasn't the answer he'd wanted but after a moment's thought he accepted the deal. "My fate lies in your hands."

"And ours in yours," said Nicholas.

"Come," Zany grabbed the cord that held the creature secure in the net and began to drag it behind him out of the door, only to stop abruptly. "The tether!" he cried. "It needs to be cut." He dropped the cord and headed back toward the chest that the net had come from and reached in.

Linny was expecting him to pull out some weird and wonderful tool, a bit like Luke Skywalker's light sabre. When he produced a large pair of shears, her eyes narrowed.

"The simple ways are usually the best," Zany

informed her. He approached the demon and began to snip the air around it.

Maybe it was her imagination, but Linny felt something tug inside her, and then release. As if she truly had been tethered to the incubus by some invisible yoke and now she was free.

"Nicholas…" she gasped.

"You're free?" He touched her cheek with a trembling hand. "You're free."

"There! All done!" Zany smirked and laid the shears aside.

"If I'd known it was that easy I could have done it myself," Linny muttered, but the truth was she felt lightheaded with relief. *She was free.* Now they just had to escape this place together, in one piece.

They headed back to the room with the void, only this time when they stepped through the door it was no longer empty. Her eyes widened as she came to a stop.

Half a dozen men sat slumped, chained against the left hand wall. Their shoulders were stooped, their heads bowed, and they looked completely exhausted in both mind and body. Linny eyed them cautiously as they shuffled their feet out of the way, chains clanking, so that Zany could get past with his captive. She noticed that despite their desperate appearance they weren't dressed like convicts. They wore a variety of outfits. One from ancient Rome, and another with a fancy ensemble that might have been in fashion when the guillotine was in use in Paris. Yet another wore a set of casual clothes Linny recognised from her own time.

That man was staring back at her. His grey hair was long and greasy, and he made her uncomfortable. She would have looked away but at that moment he spoke her name.

Startled, she stared harder. Unshaven, gaunt, his bloodshot eyes sunken in his head. Everything about him was familiar.

"Oh God." Her heart stuttered and her feet wavered. She felt Nicholas's arm slide around her waist, holding her upright.

"Linny, lass." That grating voice, as if he'd screamed so much he'd damaged his vocal cords. "Help me. Tell them it was all a mistake. Tell them I didn't mean it. Free me from this fucking place, Linny. *Please.*"

"Who is it?" Nicholas's voice was quiet in contrast, and so unlike that of the man she had hated ever since she knew what the word meant.

Somehow she managed to get the words out. "He's … my father."

That Nicholas Darlington could still be shocked by anything after the life he'd led was surprising. But she could tell he was.

She stepped out from the comfort of his arm. Her wrath held her upright now. She could have added a whole lot more to those simple words.

This is the man I wiped from my life years ago. The man who stole from me and hit me. The man who locked me up and treated me as if I was barely human. The man I wished dead over and over throughout the years, until I decided that caring even that much was not worth the effort. And yet there were times, when I was feeling par-

ticularly lonely and vulnerable, when I let myself believe that he might have changed.

"You can save me," his voice was pleading. "You owe me, lass! I'm here because of you."

Anger gave way to disbelief. "*Owe* you? How do you work that one out?" He was a pitiful creature but she would not let herself feel sorry for him.

"You wouldn't loan me that money. You had plenty and you wouldn't give me a penny. What sort of daughter does that? It's *your* fault I had to go out on the street to find some to repay the dealers. It's your fault the boy died."

He'd killed someone over a drug debt and he was blaming *her*? She shouldn't have been surprised or even disappointed. He hadn't changed. He was the past and she had moved on. She repeated it like a mantra.

"This man has failed his last chance at redemption," Zany spoke, his curious gaze switching between Linny and her father. "They all have. Now they are on their way to the underworld to receive eternal punishment."

One of the prisoners wailed like a dog, and the others echoed it. Only her father remained silent, staring her down with blazing eyes. Blaming her for his own failings.

"You *owe* me—" he rasped again, but Linny had had enough.

"You are an evil man." Her voice shook. "You treated my mother like a punching bag, and you locked me up for hours in that cupboard. But you didn't get your hands on Maggie, at least I made sure of that. And why did you treat us like that? So that you could pump your veins with drugs and spend your life high?"

"He locked you up?" Nicholas growled under his breath. She didn't look his way, though she could imagine the expression on his face.

Her father huffed, staring at Nicholas. "And who is *he*? Is this your special man? Is this the best you could do? I can tell a bad 'un, lass, and he looks like a real bad 'un." He laughed crazily.

"He's nothing like you!"

"You've never understood me, and you've never been a proper daughter. This is all your fault."

"Enough." Zany spoke with surprising authority. He dragged the incubus in its net toward the void, while it snarled and struggled, causing the line of men to pull themselves back as far as their chains would allow. A moment later he tossed it into the void, releasing the net at the same time. The inky blackness rippled, as if someone had thrown a stone in a pond, before settling again.

"Is that where we have to go?" Linny asked him shakily. "Please tell me it's not."

"No. The portal is not here, pretty lady. I will take you to it in a moment."

"Where are you going, Linny?" Her father's sneering voice made her skin prickle. "Not so bloody perfect now, are you?"

Linny glared down at him. All of her fury had seeped out of her, leaving only cold, hard contempt. "Where am I going?" she said. "I'm going home while you're going to hell. What does *that* tell you?"

He stared back at her. His lips moved but no sound came from them. For a moment she felt some pity trying to poke through the stony ground, but she refused to give it purchase. Her father didn't deserve anything more from her.

"Go now," Zany said in that same commanding voice he'd used before. "Down to the underworld where you belong."

She expected the men to protest but obediently they climbed to their feet, and began to shuffle forward. One after the other they stepped silently into the void, allowing it to swallow them. Her father didn't even look back at her as he went through, and a moment later it was as if he had never been.

She thought she should have felt something, but years of mistreatment had numbed her ability to do so.

"Now," Zany rubbed his hands together. "The portal. Your portal. I seem to remember it was this way."

"Is this how I got here last time?" Linny asked uneasily. "Is this all Stewart's doing?"

Zany shot her a look without answering, which she decided was answer enough.

He took them back into the corridor, moving quickly now, seeming to count his steps. Abruptly he stopped and looked up. Linny looked up too, and saw a shadow like a murky stain against the ceiling.

"Ah. There it is. When I call it down you must step inside," Zany instructed them. "Quickly, before

Sigurd returns. There's no time to lose."

Nicholas watched her intently. "Linny? Are you ready?"

She nodded. "Yes. Are you?"

He smiled. "Are you asking if I want to stay here, when I have the chance to return to the mortal world with you? More than ready."

Zany clapped his hands and the shadow began to move toward them. It was spinning, with dark threads woven through it.

Linny remembered a time travel series she had begun to watch on television, back before real life made it seem irrelevant. "Wait," she cried breathlessly. "Do I ... should I think of a place or a person, when I step in?"

Zany smiled. "Think of home, pretty lady. That should do it."

Nicholas held out his hand. "Come." Without hesitation she clasped his fingers in hers, and stepped into the spinning shadow.

———◆———

Home, she was thinking of home. But her father's presence had confused her, stirring up memories that crowded into her mind. Home was so many things. And Nicholas, he was her home too.

Home.

The sickening turning went on and on, and at some point her fingers slipped from his, and she was alone, tangled in the darkness.

Chapter Twenty-Two

"LINNY?"

She could smell the sea and beneath her body was hard ground with a covering of springy vegetation.

"Linny?"

His voice was an echo inside her head. A dream? Maybe it had all been a dream and none of this had happened after all. Like some B-grade movie, she was going to wake up and smile and go about her life. She and Nicholas, on the bed in the Dark World, and all she had felt when he kissed her and touched her, had just been the most epic fantasy ever. And Linny had had a lot of fantasies over the years.

Then again the lips she felt on her cheek were warm and real, and the fingers brushing back her long hair, they were real too. Those lips were closing in on her mouth, nibbling at the edges, then a tongue dipped between her lips. Now *that* wasn't a dream.

Her eyes opened.

Nicholas was crouched over her, so close she could see every dark speck in his brown eyes, his loose hair making a cage around them. She remembered she'd stolen the ribbon he normally used to tie it back. She wasn't sure why, just that at the time she had needed something of his.

He looked relieved to see her awake, his hands cupping her face, keeping her close.

"There you are," he whispered.

She blinked, expecting him to vanish, but he was still there. Suddenly everything came rushing into her head like an express train. The portal. Muddled thoughts of home. Where was she? She struggled to sit up and he leaned back onto his heels as she looked around at green hills and grey cliffs and a stormy sea.

This wasn't home. She had tried to visualise her house in Glasgow but this certainly wasn't it.

"Where are we?"

"Not sure," he said, with a half-smile. "Scotland, I think. I don't know what year though, which is a tad worrying. I don't want to suddenly be attacked by Scots."

Linny stood up, finding her feet, aware of her wobbly legs and shaky body. Her head was woozy but beginning to clear, probably because of the freezing air. Nicholas was right, this did look like Scotland, but it wasn't somewhere she recognised. More worryingly, for an urban girl like her, there didn't seem to be a city or town in sight. The sea went on endlessly, with no boats, and the sky was free of planes or any indications that one had flown overhead recently. Was Nicholas right? Were they way back in the past?

A sharp breeze blew in from the sea, making her shiver despite her coat. Nicholas stood up and put his arm around her, his hand heavy against her hip. He had become very handsy lately, and she liked it. She liked it a lot.

"We seem to be a long way from anywhere," she said, trying not to panic, and turned to look inland. With relief she spied a faint trail of smoke coming from behind the closest hill, as if from a flue, per-haps a house that was hidden from sight. "Should we go and see if we can find someone to ask?"

He looked toward the smoke and narrowed his eyes. The breeze blew his hair into his face and he had to pull it back. He glanced at her, hesitated, and said quietly, "I seem to have lost my cane."

For a moment she didn't understand and then she remembered. His leg.

"Well I'm not leaving you so you'll have to keep up," she said in her bossy voice.

He looked at her in surprise, and then smiled. He held out his hand and together they set off.

It was further than it looked, probably because there was no actual path. The hill wasn't steep, but it took time for Nicholas to negotiate the rough patches of ground. More than once, Linny had to bite her lip and look away, afraid she was going to start fussing. He wasn't the sort of man who would take fussing well. But when he stumbled for the umpteenth time and almost fell, she stepped in and grasped his arm to prevent him from taking a tumble.

His cool, "Thank you," was followed by, "You can still leave me."

"Like you left me in the Dark World?" she scoffed, and no more was said.

The house was nestled below the other side of the hill. Once they crested it, they stopped to rest. Back the way they had come was a spectacular view of the sky and sea, while across the roof of the house was more land, which ended in yet more sky and sea. The horizon was a little misty, and maybe there was something out there, but Linny couldn't see it. This seemed to be an island. It was also familiar.

Linny stared, a little frown between her brows. "I know this view."

Nicholas was breathing heavily. His leg must be hurting like crazy but he hadn't complained, and barely paused for rest, even when she'd insisted on it. Last night she'd finally seen his scars, the unsightly marks where his leg had been broken and badly set. She hadn't stared too long, she knew he didn't want to talk about it. He believed himself to be ugly, when that couldn't be further from the truth.

She told herself there would be plenty of time to draw him out, to find out why he believed the Sorceress's punishment was just, and why Sigurd had wanted him imprisoned him in the Dark World, spinning in one of those awful cages. What if it was something unforgiveable, what then? Over the years she had learned that sometimes ignorance was bliss. Did she even want to know?

His voice startled her from her thoughts. "You recognise this place?"

"I think we're on Moyle," she said. "The island Simon wrote his book about. I think we're on Simon's island."

Nicholas looked out to the sea again. "Moyle?"

She spun around, her arms spread wide. "I've seen pictures of it, but I've never actually been here. Maggie has. Maybe she's here too?"

He looked at her sharply, probably worried she was going to go into meltdown again. "What makes you think that?"

"Zany told me to think of home, right? So why did we end up here? This isn't home. I've never been here, but Maggie has. I got all muddled up thinking about what 'home' even was. Growing up, home was wherever me and Maggie were together. Maybe it brought me to her?"

Nicholas remained in silent thought. "I think we're here because Stewart wants us to be," he said at last. "We followed him from Glasgow up the coast to Port Finlay, always heading north, and now we are here on Moyle."

"But why?" she said. "How could he know we would go through the portal and end up here? Stewart wasn't there!"

"But Zany was," Nicholas said softly, "and Zany is his creature."

Linny shivered. The cold seemed to be seeping into her bones, and with it a sense of foreboding. "You mean it was all some kind of setup?"

Nicholas nodded. "I think Stewart intended us

to come to Moyle all along. This is where he plans to have his final showdown with Lorne. This is where he will attempt to destroy us all."

"I hate this," she whispered. "I just want it all to be over. I want to see my sister safe."

Nicholas wrapped his arms around her and held her close. She let the feel of him soak into her, finding comfort in it. A seabird shrieked high above, riding the wind currents.

Linny tipped back her head to look at him. "Do you think Maggie and Lorne are already here?"

"I don't know, but I do think we need to be very careful."

He looked down at her for a moment, and then bent his head and kissed her. A soft, caring kiss, that soon turned wild and passionate.

"Woman," he groaned. "Let's find a bed."

She laughed, startled. "Is this what you call being careful?"

His lips curved into a wide smile and for a moment he looked young and carefree. Then he seemed to remember where they were and why, and he wasn't smiling any more.

"You know … sometimes careful is overrated," she added, wanting to see that look on his face again. But instead of answering, he reached for her hand, taking it in his usual possessive grip.

They set off down the hill.

Chapter Twenty-Three

NICHOLAS CONSIDERED THE BUILDING TO be more of a cottage than a house. White washed stone sunken into the landscape, and despite the more modern-looking glass windows and expansion to one side, the original cottage might have been here for centuries.

He followed Linny down the path to the front door. The garden seemed to consist of metal sculptures—strange green creatures of weathered copper that Nicholas eyed uneasily. He noted a two headed dragon and wild animals with human faces. He had seen enough bizarre things of late. Give him a cat or dog any day.

Strings of sea shells hung from the eaves, twisting in the breeze that found its way into the sheltered aspect. It reminded him uncomfortably of the spinning cages in the Dark World.

At least the incubus was gone, and now Linny could sleep with a degree of safety. He felt a wave of relief that he had done that for her. As for Zany's likely deception and the portal … he wasn't happy it had taken them to Moyle, if indeed that was where they were. He believed it had been Stewart's intention all along to lead them here, from the moment he turned up at the university in Glasgow, masquerading as Simon, to their arrival in Port Finlay. Using Simon's body was the key, to give them a reason to look to his old haunts for clues, so that in time this would be where they ended up. Had they not taken this route to Moyle, Stewart would have lead them down another that ended up at the same place.

And where were Lorne and Sutcliffe? They needed to be together. That was when they were at their best, and defeating Stewart would demand them to be at their very best.

Linny was worried about Maggie, but his main concern right now was Linny herself. What if Stewart was not done plotting to hurt her? Nicholas had been prepared to give up his life for hers in the Dark World, and had assumed Linny would have been safe if Nicholas had been removed from the equation. But to have escaped that appalling place and be here with her now ... well, it was a miracle. Wasn't it?

If Stewart's plan had been to keep him banished to the Dark World, it wouldn't have been hard for Zany to prevent him from leaving. Maybe allowing them to escape and think they were safe was part of his plan. He had them believing they were on solid ground when in fact they were teetering on the edge of another chasm. And this time there would be no coming back.

"There's someone home."

Linny's voice interrupted his dark thoughts. She stepped up onto the porch, where an outdoor sofa was pushed up against the wall, covered in cushions and a blanket, all of them in striking colours. He wondered how many days of the year its occupier sat there and enjoyed the view without freezing.

Not many, he decided glumly.

"What are we going to say?" Linny asked him, her sparkling eyes lifting his mood. "Hello, we've just arrived by magic portal from the Dark World. Can you tell us where we are?"

She seemed to be inclined to giggle and when he lifted his face to the heavens it only made her worse. "At least we haven't slipped too far into the past," he said, nodding at a security camera above the door.

"Nice deduction, Sherlock. But the LED porch lights were the giveaway for me. Still, I wonder why they need that? How much crime do you get on this isolated island?" She turned back to the door. "Go on then. Knock and get this over with."

He had raised his hand to do so when the door opened.

The woman who stood there had auburn hair that hung below her shoulders, and her eyes were green. She was as tall as him, probably his age, and the smile she gave him was pretty but with an inquiring edge to it. He suspected she didn't get many visitors, and certainly not unexpected ones. Or perhaps it was him—his scar could give people a bad first impression.

"I'm sorry to intrude," he began in his most polite manner.

Linny interrupted. "We seem to be lost. We were going for a hike and it was so beautiful that we … well, I think we're lost. Can you tell us how to get back to town?"

The woman's green eyes warmed. "If you can call it a town," she said in a posh English accent, almost as posh as his own. Given her appearance and location, he had expected her to be Scottish. "Not that I'm complaining. I moved to Moyle to get away from the rat race."

They both stared at her, and Nicholas knew he was trying to decide whether or not she was real or another of Stewart's tricks. Or another skin suit he was wearing.

"I can see the attraction," Linny said with a friendly smile. "I'm Linny McNab, by the way." She nudged Nicholas.

"Nicholas Darlington." He only just stopped himself from bowing out of habit, mainly because Linny had grabbed his arm and squeezed a warning.

"Alison MacDonald-Ellis," the red head said. So, despite the accent there was certainly Scottish in her. "Would you like to come in? Maybe you can help me with a small problem I seem to have acquired. Well, a rather *large* problem, really." She seemed suddenly flustered.

"Um, sure. If we can…" Linny glanced over her shoulder at Nicholas as they followed Alison inside the cottage.

The front room was small, cosy, and warm. A fire burned in a glass-fronted box, and on a nearby sofa was a basket full of balls of wool. A half knitted garment lay tossed to one side, presumably by Alison when she came to answer the door. There were shelves with similar garments, folded and stacked. One was lying across a table, a sweater with an intricate pattern woven into it in colours of soft mauve and blue.

Linny paused to admire it. "Do you own a shop?" she said. "This is gorgeous."

"I sell online," Alison explained. "I have a small group of talented women who knit for me and I pay them. Pay them well," she added firmly, as if she'd been accused of exploitation in the past. "I'm a novice myself, but I love the process. And it gives me something to do when the weather is foul. Which it often is on Moyle."

Linny glanced at Nicholas again. *Moyle.* She was right, and now there were more questions than either of them could answer. If Stewart was involved, then their troubles were only just beginning. At the same time, if Stewart was involved, then he doubted he planned for them to suffer alone. He would want Lorne and Maggie here with them first. He was familiar enough with Stewart by now to know that he was nothing if not theatrical, and his grand finale would require the entire audience to be present.

Linny seemed lost in thoughts of her own, and Nicholas cleared his throat and turned to Alison. "What is this problem you mentioned?"

Alison had been watching him, her gaze had slid over him from head to toe, and now that she was caught out, colour crept up her neck. "Oh, yes. My problem." Nervously she tucked her hair behind her ear.

Linny moved closer to him as if staking her claim. It had been a while since any woman had done that, and it did not displease him. She frowned at him. If they'd been alone he would have kissed that frown away.

"This way," said Alison. "He's out the back. Or, at least, I think it's a 'he.'"

Together they followed her into a small kitchen and then an even smaller laundry. The back door led to an enclosed yard that ended at the side of the hill. He was just thinking how much colder it was since they were last outside, when something launched itself at him and knocked him flat.

———◆———

Nicholas looked up at the sky, and the face of a very excited dog: Loki.

He was wild with joy, jumping all over him, licking his face and making that strange wolf noise he only made for his very best friends.

Linny wasn't helping. "Loki!" she cried as she wrapped her arms around the big dog, crooning to him and raining kisses on his furry face. Behind her he saw Alison's surprised expression melt into laughter.

"He looks a bit like a wolf," she said, "but there

is nothing like that on Moyle. And he's so friendly, not savage at all."

Nicholas rolled the dog off and struggled to his feet. Using his hands to pin the wriggling Loki down, he said, "How did he get here?"

"Is he yours?" Alison asked, her face pink with laughter. "Oh, I'm so glad. I was starting to get seriously worried. He just turned up at the door yesterday and seemed so desperate to get inside. I didn't know what to do. I tried to shoo him away but he wasn't having any of that."

Nicholas laughed. "No, I'm sure he wasn't. Loki likes his own way. But he's not—"

"Yes," Linny interrupted. "He *is* ours. Thank you so much. As well as getting lost on the island we lost our dog. I apologise, Miss MacDonald-Ellis, for any trouble he's caused you."

Alison seemed to sense something amiss, but she was so pleased to have found Loki's owners that she didn't want to question them further. Nicholas could imagine that for some, having a dog like Loki in a tiny backyard was a little more than they could handle.

"Oh, what a relief. I have a cat and she hasn't been at all happy with our new arrival. I don't think your dog would hurt her but I couldn't be entirely sure. She certainly had no desire to be friends with… Loki, is it? An unusual name."

"He's named for a Norse god," Linny said, then muttered under her breath, "I'm not sure why." She grasped Loki's fur and held on. "Do you have something we can use to tie him up? That's why he escaped in the first place. His lead broke and he just took off."

"Yes, I think so." Alison turned on her heel and left them there.

When she was sure they wouldn't be heard, Linny turned to Nicholas. "Okay, what is Loki doing here? And where is Aiden? You know one is never without the other."

"They must have been separated. He must be here somewhere. We need to find him."

"Nicholas." Fear and worry shadowed her eyes. "Where's Maggie?"

"If Stewart did bring us here then he'd want all of us together. Maggie and Lorne are somewhere on this island."

"Yeah, that sounds like him. He'd want us to see how clever he is."

"Here we are!" Alison returned, holding a long thick piece of red wool in her hand, the strands knitted into a rope. "This is the best I can do, I'm afraid. I had planned to hang a potted plant from this, but hadn't got around to it yet. It's not really planting weather. Will this do?"

Linny assured her it was fine, and they proceeded to tie the rope around the dog's neck. Loki didn't seem to mind. He was calmer now. Nicholas took the other end of the improvised lead in his hand, testing it. It seemed strong enough, but Loki's exu-berance would be a test on any form of restraint.

They went to the front door, where Alison pointed in the right direction. "To reach the town you head down there. Just keep walking and you'll find a proper path. There are no proper roads on Moyle, although some of the residents have motor-cycles. When you reach the walking path, just keep following it until you come to the harbour. Are you staying at the hotel?"

"Yes," Linny said with a smile. Nicholas felt it wasn't a complete lie since that's where they would be staying now that they knew about it. "Thank you for your help."

"How long are you staying?" Alison asked.

Nicholas and Linny looked at each other. "We're not sure yet."

"Well, I assume you'll be here Saturday for the Moyle Ceilidh."

Nicholas wondered what a ceilidh was, but Linny seemed excited by the news. Although she was hiding it beneath her role as lost tourist.

"Of course I grew up in Glasgow, and although I have been to a couple, I'm sure this would be completely different."

"Oh yes, the people of Moyle have been enter-taining themselves for a very long time."

"Do they welcome outsiders?" asked Nicholas.

"They welcomed me," Alison said. "You can't get more outsider than a Londoner."

Loki began to get restless. He kept trying to turn in circles, and then tugging them back toward the cottage, where it was warm.

"We'd better go," Linny said. "Goodbye, and thank you again."

"What is a ceilidh?" Nicholas said under his breath once they were on their way. "Sounds like a form of seaweed."

Linny wasn't amused. "It's a Gaelic celebration, you Sassenach. Singing, dancing, folk music."

Before he could insult her further, Alison called out after them.

"I don't like the look of the sky. I think there's a gale coming in. You might want to hurry."

Behind them the door closed and Loki began to howl.

Chapter Twenty-Four

LINNY COULD SEE THAT LOKI wasn't happy. Whether it was the coming storm or being put in a situation he was not used to, or perhaps just missing Aiden, he was definitely not himself. The dog kept trying to turn around, struggling to look behind him, acting like he'd left something behind.

Despite Nicholas's limp, the two of them kept walking steadily in the direction Alison had provided. They soon found the walking path, which ran along the edge of the coast, sometimes climbing when there was a cliff, and then dropping to lower ground right down to the sandy beach. If they'd had more time, Linny might have let the dog take a run to burn off some energy. Then again, if they did they might never have caught him again.

"This must be an amazing place ... in the summer," she said, squinting miserably against the strengthening breeze. The weather was getting worse, the cold wind bit through their clothing and the occasional sting of salt spray on their faces.

Nicholas gave a grunt. She could see how badly

he was limping. Although she tried to take her turn with Loki, she couldn't hold him for long, and then Nicholas would have to take over. Every time Loki tugged or struggled to turn around, Nicholas's leg was jarred. Although he tried not to show it, he had to be in a lot of pain. After he had stopped and stared grimly out to sea for the umpteenth time, Linny insisted they take a break.

They had already passed a number of abandoned cottages, places that had once been inhabited by members of a busy and industrious community, but were now empty and forlorn. Some of the buildings were in better shape than others, probably used by summer visitors or campers who came to enjoy the tranquillity of the island. This was not the time of year for camping on Moyle, however, and they were all empty.

A cold gust of wind tugged at Linny's hair, almost taking her breath with it, as they reached one of the empty cottages. She informed Nicholas in her bossiest voice that they were going to stop here and take shelter.

"At least until the worst of this storm passes," she added before he could object. It said a lot about how bad he must be feeling that he nodded and followed her meekly inside.

For a moment they stood at the doorway and stared out at the wild weather and vast expanse of ocean. She could see rain moving across the surface, coming closer. They would never have found the town before they were caught up in it.

"This place is way out on the edge of civilisation," she said with a shiver that wasn't completely to do with the cold. "Imagine living here a hundred years ago? Or two? I couldn't do it. I like to have folk around me."

"You can still feel alone with people around you," Nicholas said, ignoring Loki's whining to be set free. He tethered him to a hook in what was once a fireplace.

"You think so? When Maggie was little, most of the time there was just me and her, and we had plenty of help from friends and neighbours. My dad was in and out of prison and I was always afraid some of his friends would come around and threaten me, but our neighbours kept an eye out. We might have been in the worst of places, but even then there were good people."

"I'm glad for your sake that there were." He slid down and sat on the hard-packed earth floor, stretching out his leg with a soft curse. His face looked drawn and tired, older than his years, and Linny reminded herself her Regency rake had had no sleep now for a night and a day—probably longer. Perhaps there was way to give him comfort in this bleak place?

She looked around the inside of the cottage. If she'd had her suitcase with her she would have offered him a muesli bar, but all that stuff was back in the car in Port Finlay. They hadn't had any food or drink since they'd shared the bed in the Dark World.

"Perhaps there's a tin of soup somewhere," she said.

"Or a bottle of claret." His voice was rusty, but at least he could joke. She gave him a smile as a reward for the effort.

The former inhabitants, or maybe the summer visitors, had left a large dusty box and a rickety table and chair. Linny opened the box, finding various pieces of crockery, a kerosene lamp, and a quilt inside. She lifted out the latter, trying not to think of the possibility of spiders or other crawly things, and carried it to the door. Nicholas leaned back against the door jamb, his eyes closed, so she stepped carefully over him to get outside. Some dust came out of the quilt when she shook it, and hopefully any bugs too. When she brought it back inside the cottage, she spread it out on the earthen floor.

Loki tried to claim it, but Linny shooed him away. "We should rest," she said to Nicholas. "Who knows how long the storm will last, or what might be waiting for us when we get to the harbour?"

He seemed ready to protest out of habit, but she walked over to him and bent down, brushing the back of her hand against his cheek. His eyes were a whirl of emotion. He gave up on whatever he'd been planning to say and dragged himself over to the makeshift bed. She lay down beside him, and he placed his arm around her, pulling her in against his body, so that her head rested against his chest. The quilt was big enough that they could fold it over them, like a sleeping bag. Snuggled together, they were soon nice and warm.

"Have you ever thought of getting your leg

operated on?" she said, her voice drowsy. "I know it happened a long time ago but they can do amazing things these days."

He stroked her shoulder with his fingers. "It is a reminder," he said gruffly.

"A reminder?"

"That I don't deserve to live without pain."

She wanted to tell him that was a very unhealthy attitude, but it didn't seem the right time.

Her thoughts turned to Maggie. She hoped she would see her again soon. Loki was already asleep, curled into a ball, making a little snoring noise. Nicholas's breathing slowed and evened out, even the pain of his leg couldn't keep him awake. His fingers twitched as if he was dreaming, but it wasn't a bad dream, because he settled again immediately.

Her own eyes felt so heavy. Linny smiled against the warm wool of his sweater, listening to the steady beat of his heart, and before long she had followed him into sleep.

The light was hot and bright against her eyelids. She tried to open her eyes and closed them tight again, feeling its brilliance like a spear in her brain. When she opened her eyes a second time, she squinted upwards. Her heart leapt, though she wasn't sure if it was in hope or fear.

The Sorceress stood before her, her wild red hair waving in a non-existent tempest. She smiled and Linny felt as if her heart might leave her chest entirely.

"There you are," the witch said. "Don't you two look cosy?" Her smile turned into a smug twist of her lips.

Linny tried to move but her body was locked in place, pinned by an invisible force. "Maggie," she wanted to say, hoping the Sorceress might be able to help her sister, or at least let her know what happened, but her vocal chords were locked too.

The colours around the Sorceress dimmed. "The Dark Lord and I have had words," she said. "But that does not concern you, McNab." There was a rumble of thunder far away. "That is not why I'm here."

Confused and frightened, Linny tried to turn her head, to see if Nicholas was awake as well. "You … can't take … him." She managed to force the words out, or at least she thought she did. "He doesn't deserve … be punished for something … that happened a … long time … ago. What matters is … who he is *now!*"

The witch gave a grin that was truly frightening. "Ah! You are in love with him."

Linny wanted to protest and found she couldn't. Not because of the witch, but because it was true. She *was* in love with Nicholas Darlington.

"That is good, McNab. Very good," the Sorceress almost crooned. "Nicholas deserves someone to love him. He has made great strides." Suddenly she was closer, although Linny didn't see her move. She felt as if her blood was a tide, and it was being syphoned from her body. Did the Sorceress plan to kill her? The witch's eyes were fixed on hers, and just as she had noticed with Sigurd, Linny could see movement in them, as if monsters swam deep within a vast ocean. "He hasn't told you what went before, has he?"

She shook her head. The words were only in her head but she knew the Sorceress could hear them. *I don't care, I don't need to know. It makes no difference to me.*

The witch wagged a finger. "That's all very well, McNab, but how can you give him your heart completely if you're not aware of everything he was before you found him? How can he trust you will continue to love him when his secret is always hanging over the two of you?"

"I … don't want to … know," Linny choked out. She didn't want to hear something that would turn her against him. So many men had hurt her, lied to her, tried to control her. She wanted this one to be different. Could she be blamed for hiding her head in the sand a little?

But her refusal fell on deaf ears. The awful creature in front of her had already made up her mind.

"I will show you," spoke the soft and terrifying voice. "I will lay the facts before you, so that you can make an informed decision, no matter how painful. I am going to send you back to Nicholas's time."

Was this going to be like Maggie going back to see Lorne at the Hellfire Club? No, that had been Stewart's doing, trying to drive the two apart. Maybe they were as bad as each other. Linny tried to shake her head. *No, no, no!* She tried to cling to Nicholas beside her. But it was too late. She was already spinning.

Chapter Twenty-Five

LINNY STOOD IN A SQUARE and the sun beat down on top of her bare head. She was wearing the same clothes as a moment ago, but now she felt very overdressed. As she turned to look about, Linny realized why. This wasn't Moyle during a bleak winter gale. It wasn't even Scotland. She was somewhere far warmer and more exotic.

There was a church on one side of the square, and a bell started to ring from its tower. A statue rose over a fountain, and nearby a woman was selling flowers. Narrow alleyways brought people into the square and out again, and there were children playing games on the church steps.

She heard a rumble behind her and turned to see a man with a hand cart hurrying toward her. His clothing was old-fashioned, and he wore sandals on his brown, dusty feet. He headed straight for her, but she stayed put, assuming he would go around her. He didn't. Before she could jump out of the way he had pushed his cart right through her and out the other side.

Linny stumbled and almost fell. Her bones felt jarred, her flesh shaken, as if everything inside her had been rearranged.

He'd walked *through* her!

A child came skipping toward her and this time Linny made sure to scoot out of his way. After that she decided that her boots weren't made for cobbles. Carefully, she picked her way over to the wall of the church and stood there in the shadows, relieved to be out of the hot sun. She needed to consider her surroundings, and what awfulness she might soon be involved in. The Sorceress had sent her here because she wanted Linny to know why she had taken Nicholas to the between-worlds, and why he had caught Sigurd's attention.

Looking out over the square, Linny knew she was in Italy, sometime in the past. She remembered Nicholas had said this was where his leg had been broken and his face scarred, and he'd made it clear that those wounds were tied to his sins. The scene was set.

She didn't want to be here, but the witch had left her no choice. She was about to see for herself what heinous act had been perpetrated by the man she loved.

The bell stopped ringing. It was afternoon and things had quietened down. Perhaps people were going home for a lie down before everything livened up again in the evening. She had been to Rome for a weekend once and remembered that much about their culture.

The sound of laughter caught her attention.

One of the voices sounded familiar. Linny's eyes scanned the edges of the square until she found its source. There was a bar, and at the front were awnings strung up to shade the occupants from the hot sun. Four men were seated at the only table. Even from a distance she could tell they were tipsy, if not outright drunk. Your typical tourists looking for a good time.

One of the men was Nicholas.

Unable to help herself, she drew closer. She had never seen him without his scar, and here he was, his face smooth and unmarked by suffering. And younger, because this was some years before the Hellfire Club.

When she reached him, she felt a sense of cautious relief. This didn't seem so terrible. Nicholas was happy, he was enjoying himself with his friends. He sat confidently with his shirt rumpled, untied at the throat, and she could see the warm tones of his broad chest.

Linny was about to join in with them, even knowing they couldn't hear her, when the woman arrived. They all seemed to know her, but it was Nicholas' thigh she perched on, as if she belonged there. Her dark hair tumbled loose over her shoulders and her dark eyes smouldered, while her bare feet slid up and down Nicholas's trousers.

Linny's felt a wave of jealousy, despite knowing this was so far in the past. But she *was* jealous and part of her wanted to stake her claim on him.

The woman was kissing his jaw now, her fingers tangled in his loose hair. He grinned at her, leaning in to return her kisses. His friends made silly jesting noises, but Linny's hands were clenched into fists. "Get your filthy hands off him," she growled.

She reached out to shove the woman, but of course her hand went right through, and no one even noticed. It was torture. But this couldn't be what the Sorceress had wanted to show her. She wasn't *that* big of a bitch, was she? And Nicholas and this woman canoodling was hardly serious enough to put him in line for a spin in one of Sigurd's cages.

She was so focused on the scene before her that she didn't see the two new arrivals until they were already at the table.

A young mother wearing a vermillion skirt and holding the hand of a small child stood to the side, observing the scene and yet not a part of it. At first Linny wondered whether they were curious bystanders, but there was something about the way the mother's gaze was riveted on Nicholas. The way she held her child's hand…

Linny began to feel queasy.

Nicholas had finally noticed them. Or, perhaps, realized they weren't going to go away until he did. She saw his happiness morph into a frown. "What do you want?" he said coldly.

She tried to remind herself again that this was not the man she loved. The Nicholas Linny knew would never have spoken to anyone like that. Especially if she was right about why the woman was here.

The woman said something Linny did not understand. The expression on her face was resigned. Sad. The combination did not seem to be a healthy one. Why wasn't she angry? It seemed clear enough that the woman and the child belonged to Nicholas. Because he had never said anything about having once been married, then this must be an unwed mother and her bastard. Nicholas's bastard. Why wasn't she demanding he get rid of the slut on his knee and behave himself? That's what Linny would have done.

And yet as angry as it made her to see the man she loved behaving so despicably, this couldn't possibly be the reason for Nicholas's damnation. She swallowed, wishing she could pour herself a drink from the jug on the table, because now she was wondering how much worse things were going to get.

"What are you doing here?" Nicholas asked, his frown now changing to a scowl.

The mother turned away, but Linny could see she looked even more resigned. Sorrow weighed upon her shoulders. The child swung on her mother's hand, thumb in its mouth. For a moment it seemed as if Nicholas was going to smile, maybe even beckon the child forward. Then the slut on his lap whispered in his ear and Linny could see how easily he was persuaded to change his mind. The moment passed.

Nicholas made an impatient sound, and reaching into his pocket he found some coins and tossed them onto the cobbles in front of her. They rolled and scattered, glinting dully in the sunlight. His companions roared with laughter, and raised their mugs to Nicholas as if he had done something amusing. The woman plastered on his knee giggled and ran her fingers through his hair, as if to rub salt into the wound.

The mother stared at Nicholas a moment longer and Linny could see some other emotion had joined the resignation and the sorrow. Determination. She didn't bend to pick up the coins, but instead tightened her grip upon the child's hand and walked away.

Linny watched them go. The woman wore shoes and her dress was, as far as Linny could tell, well made for the time. No patches or darns, certainly not the rags she had seen some of the other women in the square clothed in. This was no beggar. She didn't need the coins, and the throwing of them had been meant to insult her.

Linny turned to look back at the man she loved. Or, at least, the ghost of that man's past. He hadn't noticed the pair walk away because he was too busy enjoying himself.

"Go after her," Linny said. Leaning closer she pressed her mouth to his ear. "Go after her, you bloody selfish tosser!"

He didn't hear her.

Linny wanted to shake him and tell him off, but it was pointless. He couldn't hear her and this had all happened a long time ago.

Her feeling of foreboding grew stronger as she reminded herself that there was nothing she could do to change the past. She was an observer, and a reluctant one. And the worst was surely still to come.

Nicholas had gone back to his carousing and Linny had seen enough. She hurried after the mother and child, avoiding another handcart and a group of youths who seemed more interested in looking cool than watching where they were going. Not that they could have seen her, but she suspected it wouldn't have made much of a difference if they could.

She spotted the pair at the edge of the square, where an arched entrance led out onto a dock. Breathless by the time she reached the arch, Linny stopped to watch the little boats rocking at their moorings. The scene was a peaceful one. But the pair were not to be seen.

Some of the fishermen were calling out to passers-by—shop keepers and housewives. When someone stopped there was much bartering and a great deal of play acting. The fishy smells made Linny's nose twitch, and then she saw the mother further down the quay.

The child was barely at walking stage, with dark hair and delicate features. And yet there was something about her that made Linny think she was Nicholas's daughter. This woman was his convenient mistress, if the scene she had just witnessed was anything to go by. That he had treated anyone in that dismissive, cruel manner, made Linny feel ashamed of him.

Was she meant to be impartial? The Sorceress had wanted all the facts laid before her, so that she could make an informed decision. But nothing was quite that simple. And surely this alone couldn't be what the Sorceress wanted her to see. Bad as this was, it was not the stuff of eternal damnation.

Lost in her thoughts it took a moment before she realised she had again lost sight of the pair. The crowd seemed to have grown, and the shadows were longer. Nap time was over. Linny was still trying to find them in the noisy crowd, when it occurred to her they may have gone back to the square.

There was a shout from the direction of the boats. And then a scream.

Linny began to run. She felt her body being pushed and pummelled as she ran through people. The sensation was unpleasant and unsettling and to stop herself from falling she eventually had to cling to a pole used as a mooring to get her balance.

She saw something in the water. A vermillion skirt spread out across the surface. One of the fisherman had a pole with a hook on the end, and he tried to snag the rapidly vanishing cloth, but it was too late. In barely a moment, the clothing had become heavy enough to take the body inside it down, and the water was smooth and empty again. It was just as if nothing had ever happened.

Linny stared in disbelief. Surely the child was still here somewhere? She swung around, and then fell as someone else rushed through her. She sat on the grubby cobbles and only then realised that there were tears streaming down her cheeks.

She lost track of how long she sat there. People

in the crowd called for help, and someone dove into the water. More fisherman gathered, and those who were able, jumped into the water to assist. Eventually two bodies were hauled up onto the dock. I appeared that the mother had something tied about her waist, a rope attached to a weight that had perhaps been cast aside from one of the boats. Enough to ensure she could not be saved when she jumped into the water.

There was no dignity in death, but some of the onlookers did their best, laying the pair of them neatly side by side.

That was when she heard Nicholas's voice.

He was drunker than he'd been when she last saw him. His hair was in disarray and his shirt partially untucked from his trousers. His feet were bare. He took a few wavering steps closer and she could see the wildness in his eyes, the grief and regret. He fell to his knees.

It tore her heart in two seeing him like this, but she couldn't look away. This was a man she hadn't known. This Nicholas was a stranger to her, but she was witnessing the event that had made him who he was now. The horrifying moment that had brought him into the realm of the Sorceress and the Dark Lord.

A man abruptly appeared at his shoulder, taking both Linny and Nicholas by surprise. His face was almost as grief stricken as Nicholas's. He didn't speak but struck Nicholas across the face, sending him sprawling.

The man spoke with a low voice, throbbing with

emotion. Stunned, Nicholas scrambled awkwardly
to his feet. He was still unsteady but his jaw was
hard and set, as if he had made up his mind. He
nodded a reply to the man's question. The man
stared at him a moment longer, then spat on the
ground at his feet, and walked away.

It was the prelude to a duel. This would be how
Nicholas received the scar on his face. At this
moment, she could see that he felt he deserved
whatever happened to him now.

He was hoping he would die. Only death was
punishment enough for the pain he had inflicted
on this day.

Chapter Twenty-Six

NICHOLAS TUCKED THE QUILT AROUND Linny. A moment ago she had shivered, and he became aware of the air turning colder. The storm had passed, but it had left an icy chill in its wake. Moyle was not the place he would have chosen to visit at this time of year, but then they had no say in the matter. If it wasn't Stewart then it was the Sorceress who ruled their lives.

He reached out and tucked Linny's hair behind her ear, enjoying the warmth of her body against his. This was a moment he had never thought he would have with any woman. And even if the chance had come he would have turned his back on it, believing he did not deserve it.

He wasn't sure he would ever truly believe he deserved to be happy. He would always strive to be a better man, although he sometimes wondered if he could achieve it. And yet here, now, with Linny in his arms, he felt a new sense of peace.

A tear ran down her cheek and she opened her eyes.

Nicholas frowned, half sitting up. "Linny?"

She burrowed her face deeper into his chest and he heard her sob. He had a sick feeling in his stomach. Something was wrong, and he suspected it wasn't just a bad dream. "Linny, what is it?"

She shook her head, but he needed to know. She was shaking, her skin clammy, and he thought she might be unwell. Immediately his brain began working out how he could find a physician, or how he could get her to the town as quickly as possible.

"You threw them away," she said, and looked up at him.

He stared at her, a frown between his brows. For a moment he didn't understand. *Threw them away?* And then he saw the agony in her eyes, and realized what she meant.

"You threw them away," she repeated. "As if you'd never loved them at all. As if they meant nothing to you."

His chest felt as if a hand was slowly squeezing his heart to a stop. He hunched his shoulders, his hand covering his face. "I see. You know," he said, his voice shaken. "How…?"

Linny's voice grew husky as she struggled to force the words past the lump in her throat. "The witch showed me. I was there. I *saw*, Nicholas."

He groaned and knelt beside her, head still bowed, eyes closed and silent. Every breath he took hurt. She knew, and now she could not help but loathe him as much as he loathed himself.

"Why didn't you tell me?" She tried to lift his face with her hands, but he couldn't have her touch him. He couldn't let her contaminate herself with his wickedness. He pulled away.

"Why?" He stood up and turned his back. Better she didn't see how much of an effort it was to keep such violent emotions in check. "You saw the man I was!"

"Nicholas..." It was barely a whisper.

"I was a cunt." He spat the word out. "A bastard with no heart and conscience. I am a murderer, Linny. Oh, I may not have put them in the water, but I might as well have filled their pockets with rocks."

For a moment she didn't move. He half expected her to walk out of the door, to get as far away from him as possible.

"You did do a terrible thing," she said, slowly getting to her feet. Her fingers brushed his shoulder and slipped away again. "But you're not that man any more. You haven't just been punished all this time, you've repented. Oh God, have you repented. You've been to hell and back."

He shook his head, his hands on his hips. "It's not enough," he said in a low voice. "Not nearly enough. Don't you understand now why Sigurd wanted me in his realm ... because I believe I belong there."

"So you want to spin in one of those cages we saw? Would that make you feel better?"

Despite the ache in his chest, her tone surprised him. He'd been expecting anger and hurt, and certainly disgust. But irritation? He turned to her, answering in a voice that was almost normal. "Not even that would be enough."

Her dark eyes softened. "That's the problem, isn't it? You believe you deserve punishment, and that belief trumps all evidence to the contrary. You can't be forgiven until you can forgive yourself. Acceptance has to come from inside, and I think you are ready for that, Nicholas. I do. My father threw us away too, Maggie and me, and he was never sorry. Not once. You saw him ... you heard him. Right up till the end, he still blames me for what he did, and he will never change. You're not like that."

He wiped a hand across his mouth. She was trying so hard to make him see that he deserved forgiveness. "Being a slightly better man than your father is not exactly praise worthy, Linny," he said, sadness in his brown eyes.

"The Sorceress thought you were worth saving," she retorted, and stepped so close they were nearly touching. "Your friends think you are worth saving. *I* believe you are worth saving. Why shouldn't you think it of yourself?"

He stared at her, trying to picture the man she was seeing before her. He remembered their encounter with her father and she was right—that wasn't a man who would ever admit he was at fault. That wasn't someone who could ever be saved.

But Nicholas wasn't that man. He had admitted his faults, over and over. He fought every day to be better than the day before, though he could never undo what had been done.

"You believe in me?" he said, a touch of hope in his voice.

"Yes. I do."

He searched her face and saw only truth. Her eyes filled with tears but she wiped them away. "You were horrible back then, Nicholas. That man I could never have loved. But this man here, before me … I do love him."

He bit his lip, his own eyes welling up. "You love me?" he said shakily, barely believing it. "How can you?"

She put her arms around him and pulled his face down to hers. They sank down onto the quilt, kneeling, her arms still tight about his shoulders, his face warm against her skin. He was shaking, sobs now rising from deep inside him, unstoppable. He was a broken man, and his only hope right now was that she could put him back together again.

<hr/>

Linny stroked the hair from his cheek, feeling the rasp of whiskers. He'd sobbed like a child, a purging of emotion long overdue.

"After the duel, after the shot sliced through my cheek and I lay wounded and bleeding on the ground, my opponent broke my leg. He was a cousin of the woman I …" He cleared his throat. "He was her only family and he had never approved of her liaison with me. When he challenged me to a duel I wanted him to hurt me, but this was not the sort of duel I was used to. Even my so-called friends did not care much what happened to me. Not after…" He sighed. "I was close to death.

When I came back from Italy my family disowned me, and my leg was beyond repair. I thought about letting myself die, but for some reason I chose to live."

"I'm glad."

He shook his head but she saw the barely there twitch of his mouth, trying to smile. "I went to live with Lorne and Sutcliffe, right before we formed the Hellfire Club. There, I could drink and whore myself into forgetting about the past. It was a kind of death, I suppose. I probably would have died eventually, but honestly I believed even death was too good for me."

"The Sorceress decided you were worth saving," she said, tracing the line of his scar with her finger.

"I almost wasn't," Nicholas countered. "I didn't realise what a close thing it was until Sigurd said I nearly ended up in the Dark World. Perhaps I should have, and yet…" He looked up at her, his head resting in her lap. "I'm glad I was able to be there for you."

"So am I, Nicholas."

His face cleared. "I want you to know that I will *never* stop trying to be a better man. I will never forget what I did. But if you love me, as you say you do, Linny, then perhaps I can allow myself forgiveness while still fighting for redemption. I would count my blessings every day with you, Linny. Every day."

She gazed down at him a moment, and then she bent and pressed her lips to his. "Until you," she said, "I was kind of a mess myself."

He reached up and wrapped his hand around her neck, tangling his fingers in her hair, and deepened their kiss. She climbed over him, straddling his body, and Nicholas groaned. His free hand slid down to cup her bottom through her jeans. She could already feel the swell of his cock, and it felt extremely urgent for him to be inside her.

He arched his hips as she rubbed her hand against him, and then they were fumbling to remove his pants, his need as great as hers. Linny barely had her own jeans down when her panties were pushed to one side and he thrust in.

"Oh God…" she gasped. He caught hold of her hips, holding her there, so deep inside her she felt completely full. She rested her hands on his chest, steadying herself, and saw the fire in his eyes. This need between them had to be satisfied.

It didn't take much to reach her orgasm, and he followed almost straight after, groaning out her name. She collapsed across him and nuzzled against his throat, taking in his scent.

"I love you more than life," he said, husky with emotion. "You are everything to me, never doubt it."

She stroked his jaw with a trembling smile. "I don't. I won't."

And then, suddenly aware of a new problem, she sat up and looked around.

"Where is Loki?"

Chapter Twenty-Seven

THE RED KNITTED ROPE THEY had used as a leash was broken in two, hanging limp from the hook near the fireplace, but of Loki there was no sign. They went outside and called for him, but the dog was long gone.

"Perhaps he found Aiden?" Linny suggested.

"Perhaps. Or, more likely, he's gone back to the cottage we found him in. Clever dog. Warmer there."

"Should we go back and find him?"

"I think we need to get to the town and worry about Loki later. He is used to the outdoors, and has a thick enough coat to survive this weather; we don't."

Linny agreed, and they set off along the path, trying to ignore the stinging wind and the salt spray that blew up from the sea below. Nicholas held Linny's cold hand in his, trying to instil a little bit of his own warmth into it. They didn't speak much, everything that needed to be said had been said earlier, and he felt comfortable with their current silence.

They would talk again, but for now they had said enough. She loved him. Despite everything, she loved him. He wanted to simply savour that fact.

The sky was getting darker and the wind beginning to howl, when they finally topped a rise. There before them was a small harbour and the town huddled around it. Most of the buildings were single storey, painted white and traditional looking. The only stand out was a two storey hotel, brand spanking new, set toward the back of the cluster.

"Maggie told me about that," Linny said, as they drew closer. "The locals put up a real fight against it being built, but money won out in the end. To be fair, I think they've had more visitors because of it."

"As long as it has a fire," Nicholas said, trying not to let his teeth chatter. He'd handed over his sweater to Linny some miles back, and he had been slowly freezing ever since.

Linny had offered it back but he had refused, playing the gentleman.

It was late in the afternoon now and nothing seemed to be open. The lights in the few shops were out and the 'Closed' signs were visible everywhere. This time of year there would be few enough casual visitors, and only the determined ones were here for the ceilidh.

The waves were whipping up against the jetty, making any ferry boats think twice about the journey from the mainland. Nicholas wondered how they were going to leave Moyle, but they had matters to attend to first.

More than ever he needed to deal with Stewart, clear the slate with the Sorceress, and perhaps, if he was lucky, live the rest of his life with the woman he loved.

"This must be where the ceilidh is on Saturday night," Linny said, looking up at the impressive façade of the hotel. "One way to win over the locals, I suppose."

"And warmer than one of their cottages," muttered Nicholas, and heard her giggle. They pushed open the door and stepped inside the cosy foyer.

A woman with blonde hair and tartan trousers hurried over. "Hello, hello," she said, in a voice made to carry. "Good weather for ducks out there, is it not?"

Linny smiled back, her fingers tightening in his. "Eh, it is. We're here for…"

"You're lucky you got here before the weather turned worse. Came on the chartered plane, did you? I doubt it will be returning to Glasgow tonight, so you're lucky to be here."

"Yes, the plane," Linny repeated, clearly at a loss.

"You're here for the ceilidh? We have quite a crowd in for Saturday, although some are yet to arrive. What are your names so that I can show you to your room?"

Nicholas followed the woman to the desk. It seemed the thing to do. Maybe he could bluff his way through this. Or, more to the point, Linny could. He didn't care if he took someone else's room as long as he could have a hot bath and thaw out the bits of him that needed thawing.

"Do you have a list?" he asked authoritatively.

"I do indeed." She turned the book around and he ran his eye down it. Startled, he discovered his own name already on the page. Linny came to his side and bent her head.

"That's us," she said, then tried to sound like she'd expected it to be there all along. "That's us."

"Oh, Earl Northcott!" the woman fluttered her eyelashes. "We do get a few titled gentlemen here from time to time, but to have so many at once? How exciting!"

"Who else—?" Linny began, but was cut short.

"We're booked out, so if you weren't on the list it wouldn't have mattered who you were, we would have had to turn you away." She gave a startled laugh at the look on their faces. "Only joking, I'm sure there'd be a cupboard somewhere for you. As it is, you have been allocated one of our nicer rooms."

They followed her up the stairs to their floor. She chattered continually, talking about the events planned for Saturday and how lucky they were to be here, and not to worry too much about the weather. "We'll be inside most of the time, so what does it matter what it's like outside?"

"I suppose…"

"Professor Simon Frazer's cousin will be here. I'm sure you've heard of Simon," she said with a sad smile. "He was one of Moyle's most famous sons. An acclaimed archaeologist and a great patron of our island."

Simon? Linny mouthed to Nicholas. Nicholas, however, was less surprised. They had been brought here for a reason, they had reserved rooms for a reason, and Simon's cousin—assuming it wasn't Stewart wearing another body again—was here for a reason. For now, they had to play the part they had been given, until they could get their bearings.

"Here we are." The room behind the door was indeed a nice one, very modern, with a view from the windows to the harbour and the wild weather beyond. Sleety rain lashed the thick glass and Nicholas felt glad to be on the other side. There was a queen-sized bed and a bottle of champagne in an ice bucket waiting for them.

"We will be serving dinner at six. Early hours this time of year, I'm afraid. If you need anything just pick up the phone and let me know." And with that she finally left them alone.

"Simon's *cousin*?" Linny said, her pitch rising. "Simon doesn't have a cousin. This is Stewart, isn't it? He's brought us here, and now he has us trapped."

He went to her, wrapping her in his arms. "Hush, love." He breathed in the scent of her hair. "We'll deal with Stewart when the time comes. For now, let's just be grateful to be here, safe and sound, together."

The tension left her body and with a sigh she relaxed into him. "I know we will. It just never seems to end."

"In time we will prevail. Consider the fact that both of us can sleep tonight, at the same time.

That's progress."

She lifted her chin and stared up at him, laughter sparkling in her eyes. "You're teasing me, Earl Northcott."

"Did it work?"

"Maybe." She stretched up onto her toes and kissed his lips. "I'm not sure I want to sleep, though. We have a lot of making up to do."

"That we do."

She laughed just as they heard a knock on the door.

"Oh God, what now?" Linny moaned. Nicholas put her behind him and limped to answer it. "Wait, wait," she came after him. "What if it's Stewart? Use the peephole."

If it was, the peephole would be of little use, but he did so. Satisfied, and only somewhat surprised by what he saw, he unlocked the door and flung it open.

"Maggie!" Linny shrieked and ran to her sister. They hugged and stumbled in a circle, crying out in joy. Next came Lorne, who took Nicholas's hand in a warm clasp, and then pounded him on the back.

"You're safe," Nicholas said with obvious relief.

"You too. How did you get here?"

"That will take some explaining. Where's Aiden?" Lorne's smile faded. "He isn't with you?"

"No. We found Loki, but he ran off again."

"Where there's Loki then Aiden is also," Lorne said to himself. His eyes closed for a moment. "We need to find him," he said. "If we have all been drawn to this place, then it's because Stewart is ready to make his move. If we hope to defeat him we must be united, all of us. Safety in numbers."

"One for all," Nicholas said quietly, remembering the other times they had faced danger together. "Lorne, we have to capture Stewart this time. We *have* to."

Lorne's face softened. "Don't worry, friend. We will see him locked away forever, and then…" His lips hardened. "Then I will beg for my own happiness and pray she gives it to me." He looked over at Linny and then back to Nicholas. "Am I correct in assuming I won't be alone in that?"

Nicholas smiled as Linny and Maggie joined them "No, you will not be alone."

Lorne nodded. "Then the only question left is, where is Aiden?"

Epilogue

"YOU WRETCHED DOG!" ALISON BLOCKED the doorway but Loki wasn't having any of that. He leapt up, making her step back, and before she knew it he was inside her cottage, tracking mud.

"I thought you'd gone!" she declared. She paused a moment, wondering if the couple who had taken him had found themselves in difficulty. It had been strange seeing them here in such weather. They were hardly dressed for it. She'd half wondered if they were ghosts from another time, especially the man.

Loki danced around, whining, knocking things over with his big tail. She caught him by the lead and saw that it was the same one she had given them, the impromptu knitted rope, only it had broken off and the dog was trailing a foot of it behind.

"So you ran away, you wretched animal," she muttered, tugging him toward the laundry. "Well you can stay in here. I won't have you tracking mud on my knitting, thank you very much."

The dog tried to escape, staring desperately over her shoulder. So desperate that Alison turned to look. The room was empty though, nothing to see, and with an impatient sigh she hauled the dog into the room and closed the door. Immediately, it began to scrabble on the wood with claws she knew would leave marks.

Wonderful.

She still had several garments to finish for Saturday night. The owner of the hotel had allowed her to set up a little shop in their foyer, and her team was working overtime to get everything finished. She'd been assured that the guests were well healed, so it would be worth the effort. They might do well, and word of mouth was a wonderful thing. With luck, some Facebook and Instagram buzz would put them on the map.

Loki began to howl.

Alison put her hands to her ears and groaned aloud. "Oh, come on now. Stop it!"

She turned to return to her seat by the fire, just as something brushed by her. Something big.

Alison froze. The room was empty, she could see with her own eyes that she was alone, yet there was something else in here with her. And why was the dog still howling? Did it sense whatever was here?

"Who are you?" she demanded, trying to sound calm instead of frightened out of her wits. She had had the sight since she was a child, but she had never been comfortable with it, had never wanted it. It was just something that was part of her, like the colour of her hair or eyes. Until now, her little isolated cottage had been safe from the 'others' as she liked to call those that lived in the spirit world.

"Answer me," she said, folding her arms.

Something shifted in the atmosphere. As if the air had been displaced by something very large. And then a voice spoke, although it was in her head rather than heard by her ears.

"I am Sutcliffe," it said in a deep aristocratic voice. *"Please, help me."*

Acknowledgements

My thanks go to Noah Chin, who edited this book and offered so many suggestions to make it better. To Christine Gardner whose line editing gave everything an extra polish. Thank you to my family who are always supportive and understanding, even when I'm writing at Christmas. And lastly but most important of all, thank you to my readers who continue to support me.

About the Author

Sara Mackenzie is the author of The Immortal Warriors series. She also writes Historical Romance as Sara Bennett and Evie North. You'll find all three of them here:
www.sara-bennett.com

You can visit her on her Facebook page:
www.facebook.com/saramackenzieparanormalromance

While you're there sign up to her Newsletter for the latest news:
www.facebook.com/saramackenzieparanormalromance/app/152926008054123

Look for these titles by
Sara Mackenzie

NOW AVAILABLE:
Return of the Highlander
Secrets of the Highwayman
Passions of the Ghost

Hellfire Club: Lorne (1)
Hellfire Club: Darlington (2)

COMING NEXT:
Hellfire Club: Sutcliffe (3)

CPSIA information can be obtained
at www.ICGtesting.com
Printed in the USA
LVHW011621280720
661666LV00009B/427